Shapecaster

Jennifer Stolzer

ISBN: 978-1-079-52469-7

© 2019, Jennifer RStolzer, LLC
edition 2

Illustration: Jennifer Stolzer
All rights reserved under international and pan-american copyright conventions. No part of this book may be used or reproduced in any manner.

Table of Contents

Chapter 1: Shapes..................................1
Chapter 2: The Worst Day....................8
Chapter 3: Things You Can't Draw..........16
Chapter 4: Sneaking Out.....................26
Chapter 5: Grounded........................36
Chapter 6: The New Worst Day.............49
Chapter 7: Escape!...........................59
Chapter 8: A New Plan......................69
Chapter 9: The Most Important Meeting...78
Chapter 10: Caster............................86
Chapter 11: Big Decisions...................95
Chapter 12: The Secret of the Shapes.......103

To all the kids out there who see shapes.

Sometimes what makes you different can scare you, but sometimes it can also help you.

Be brave in the hard times.
There are people around you who love you no matter what.

Chapter 1
Shapes

After Cat hit her head, she saw shapes everywhere. More than noticing that a picture frame was a square and a clock was a circle, Cat saw knots and tangles floating behind her eyelids when she closed her eyes. She dreamed about shapes. Other people looked like shapes. Words became shapes. Shapes were everywhere!

Cat watched the shapes float in her breakfast porridge at the kitchen table and tugged at the bandage wrapped around her head. Mom reached over the table and swatted Cat's hand. "Don't touch your bump."

"I wasn't!" Cat cried.

"Yes you have. You've been poking it all morning," Mom said.

"That's because it still hurts."

"Dr. Charles says you're fine," Mom said. "You've moped around all week. It's time you go back to school."

"The kids are going to laugh at me." Cat poked the bandage again. Every time she pressed on the bump the shapes danced in circles in front of her eyes.

"Stop touching it," Mom said, again. "Now go get ready."

Cat grumbled and sulked off to her room.

The first thing she did was find a hat. The second thing she did was find her homework.

Peter brought her schoolwork home to her in big stacks throughout the week. The pile of dusty textbooks teetered on the edge of her dresser, stuffed full of worksheets she was supposed to do while she was sick. Cat hadn't done any of it. It was "magic class" time of year and Cat hated magic class.

When Cat was a baby, Mom would tell

Chapter 1 - Shapes

her stories about the Holy Calligraphers. The Calligraphers were the only ones in the world with magic powers, and used their spells to keep everything running the way it was supposed to. Cat had never seen a Calligrapher in person, nor had she seen magic performed outside the dusty books. She thought it was unfair that normal people were forced to build and make things by hand when magic was available. And it wasn't fair that she had to learn about it every year either.

    Cat dove back into her closet and fished out the graded worksheets from the previous summer. Cat laid the worksheets side by side on the floor and saw the questions were the same on both. She'd only gotten a "B" on the assignments, but she was okay with a "B" two years in a row. The shapes floating around her head drifted over the pages, resting on words like "spells" and "Curses" before flitting away.

    Cheating was against the rules. Cat knew she'd get in trouble if she got caught copying her work, but it wasn't her fault the questions were the same, and it wasn't her fault that she got a bump on her head. Cat copied the answers in hurried letters and hoped Mrs. Smith wouldn't notice.

Cat stuffed the worksheets in her backpack and wedged in the text books. There were way too many to fit. She put the extra books in her pillow case and slung it over one shoulder with both hands. Cat got a look at herself in the mirror by the door and groaned.

"If they don't laugh at my bandage, they'll laugh because I look like a laundry girl with this bag," Cat said.

She said goodbye to Mom, and headed off to school. Mason Forge was a tiny mountain town. Cat could walk from one end to the other without breaking a sweat. There were two main roads that intersected at the top of the hill, and a gate that opened to a forest at the bottom. The

Chapter 1 - Shapes

buildings were made of wood and stone with lots of yard ornaments to decorate their front walks. Further up the mountain, Cat could see the fields where the farmers grew crops to feed everyone and sell in the city on the other side of the forest. Almost everyone in town grew up to be farmers.

Cat wouldn't mind being a farmer – she always liked plants – but her dad wanted her to be a lawyer like he was, and that meant even more school than normal kids. The thought of school made Cat's bump hurt. She watched the shapes dance before her eyes as she walked.

A couple of the younger kids were playing outside the school house before the bell rang. There were only ten kids in town so all of them were in the same class even if the younger kids were learning their numbers while the older kids were doing equations.

Eric stood sneering on the steps. He was a year older than Cat and a whole lot bigger. He was also her least favorite classmate.

"Hey Kitty Cat," Eric called. "What's with the bag? Are you a cat burglar?"

Cat rolled her eyes. "It's my homework."

"So what's with that ugly hat?" Eric asked.

"None of your business."

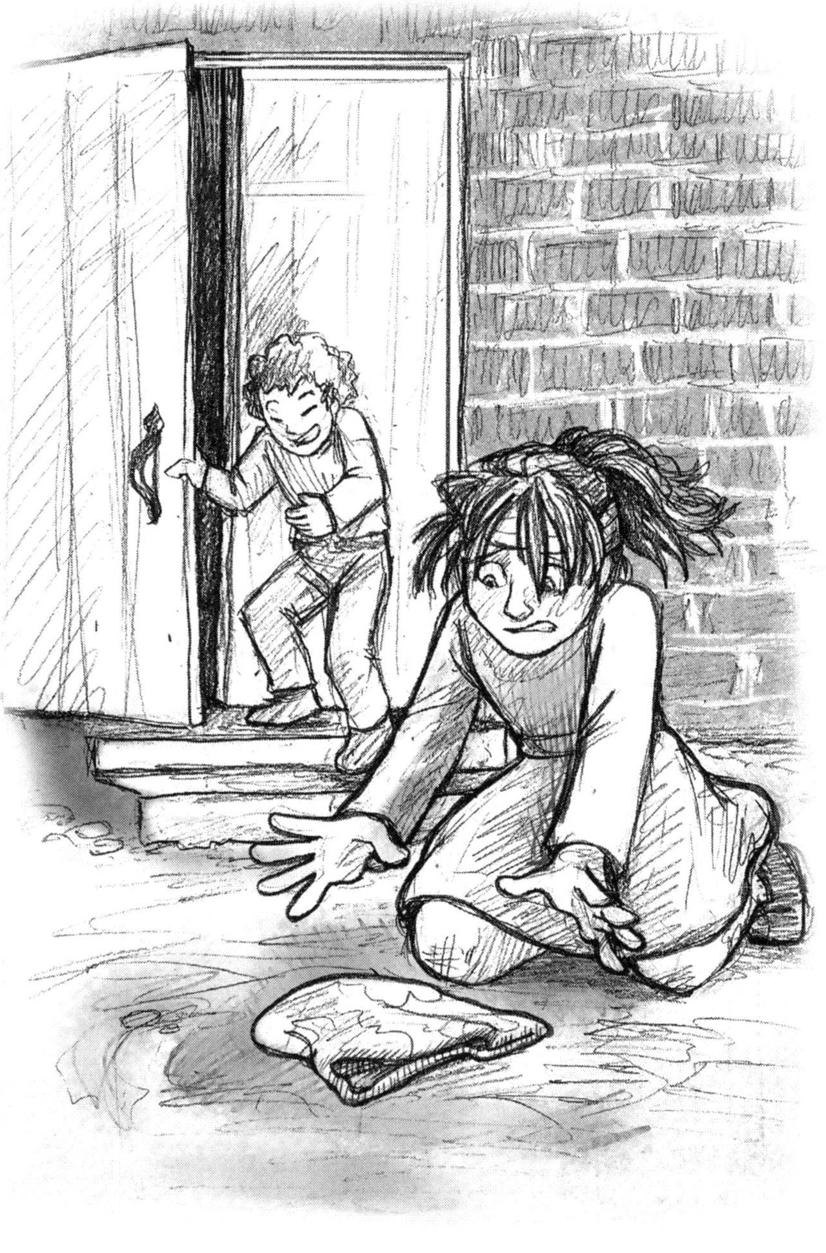

Chapter 1 - Shapes

"Oh yeah?"

Before she could drop the bag to stop him, Eric snatched the hat off her head. The other kids in the yard stared at her bright white bandage that made her brown hair stick up in all directions.

Eric laughed his donkey laugh again and pointed at her head. "You look so stupid!"

"Give it back, Eric!" Cat shouted.

The school bell rang. Eric threw Cat's hat into the street. "Get it yourself, Cat Burglar!"

Cat dropped her bag of books to grab the hat mid-air. It flew out of reach and landed like a dead fish in the dirt. The younger kids snickered and ran past her into class.

"Perfect." Cat huffed. Dust covered the knitted hat inside and outside. She saw pieces of the floating shapes repeated in the dirty patches; circles, squares, wavy lines, and loops linked together like a chain. Cat shook her head to disperse the shapes and tugged the dirty hat back on. "Better to be dirty than laughed at."

Cat picked up her pillowcase and followed Eric inside.

Chapter 2
The Worst Day

Cat's school books swam with shapes and symbols that didn't belong there. It was the same for the marks on the chalk board. Cat tried shaking her head or rubbing her eyes to get rid of the shapes. She even tried closing one eye at a time, but the shapes were clearer in the closed one than the open one.

Cat glanced over her shoulder at Peter. Her best friend sat a row behind her and to the left, his glasses reflecting the map he

Chapter 2 - The Worst Day

was drawing in his notebook. Perhaps it was another pretend treasure map the two could follow after school. The floating shapes traced the reflection of a mountain as he drew it.

"Catrina," Mrs. Smith called.

Cat sat bolt upright. "Yes?"

Mrs. Smith was frowning. "I called your name twice. Answer the question: How do the Holy Calligraphers perform magic?"

"Uh… they..." Cat tried again to read the chalkboard for clues, but there were too many shapes in the way.

"You haven't been paying attention at all," Mrs. Smith said. "A bump on the head is no excuse for not listening. I'm giving you recess detention."

Cat gasped. "That's not fair!"

"Yes it is," Mrs. Smith said. "Everyone else, it's time to play outside."

The class rushed out the back door to the playground where a metal slide and a squeaky swing waited. Cat had to sit on the bleachers while everyone else played in the yard. The other kids weren't allowed to talk to her. Peter sat on the edge of the sandbox doodling in his notebook. He waved to her. Cat made sure Mrs. Smith wasn't watching before waving back.

They hadn't hung out while she was on head-bump rest because of Dr. Charles's orders. The week was the longest time Cat and Peter had been apart for their entire lives. Friend time would have probably helped more than rest. She was dying to tell him about the shapes. Peter was the smartest kid in school, he probably knew what the shapes were and how to get rid of them, but she would have to wait until after school to talk to him.

Cat pulled off the bracelet she wore around her left wrist. It was actually a long loop of string that her mom gave her to keep her quiet during church. It worked better than Mom could have expected. Cat threaded the string around her fingers and began exchanging loops hand-to-hand, creating different patterns with each combination.

First she made the 'Cup and Saucer, then the "Calligrapher's Paintbrush." Cat pulled the knots loose and stretched the string again to begin the 'Sky Ladder.' The diamonds floating in her vision fit themselves to the shapes in the string. Cat blinked to scatter them, but they stuck like glue.

"Hey look, it's the Cat Burglar!"

Eric sauntered up with his two lackeys;

Chapter 2 - The Worst Day

another boy named Brett and a girl named Jenny. The two older kids were fine on their own, but when Eric got them all together Cat knew it meant trouble.

Eric's voice whined like a deflating balloon. "Where's your bag, Cat Burglar?"

"I was done with it so I put it away." Cat pulled her hands out of the string and started a new pattern. "You can't talk to me, I'm in detention."

"Brett and Jenny want to see what's under your hat," Eric said.

Cat pouted. "It's a bandage from when I hit my head."

"I heard it was gross and dripping with blood!" Brett said.

"I heard you can see her brains under it!" Jenny added.

Cat ignored them and concentrated on her string. Making the thread patterns calmed her, even with the throbbing bump on her head and all the floating shapes in her eyes. The world felt right when what started as a tangle stretched into something purposeful. She started the 'Sky Ladder' again. Halfway through the steps, the string knotted in the middle like cat whiskers. She smiled. Eric's hand whooshed past her face and clamped around the string.

"Hey!" Cat shouted.

Eric pulled the thread from her fingers and balled it in his hands. Cat became furious. She leaped off the bleachers. "Give it back!"

"Try and take it from me, Cat Burglar!" Eric said. He held the fist with the string up high so she had to jump to reach it.

Brett and Jenny laughed. Jenny tripped Cat's foot. Brett pushed her down. Eric, for the second time that day, stole the hat from the top of her head.

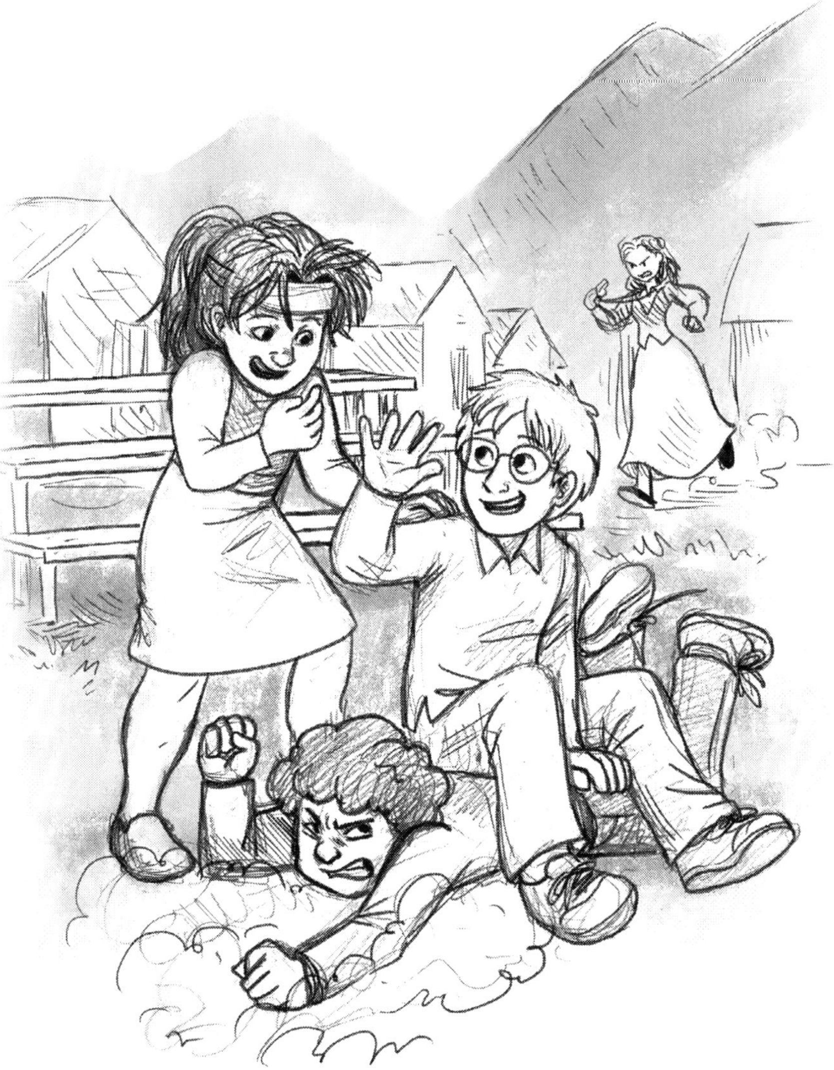

"See? Didn't I tell you it was stupid?" Eric said, but his smile vanished when he was struck without warning from behind. Eric fell flat on his face and Peter sat on his back.

Cat forgot all about her weird hair and smiled. "Peter!"

He put a finger to his lips. "You're in detention."

"Help! Help!" Eric shouted. "Mrs. Smith!"

Brett and Jenny ran for it. Mrs. Smith charged across the yard and dragged Peter off Eric by one arm. Eric sniffled as he stood. His nose was bleeding.

Mrs. Smith's face went red. "What's the meaning of this?"

"They attacked me!" Eric said. "I was minding my own business!"

"I doubt that's the whole story," Mrs. Smith said. "But that doesn't change the fact that I found you two fighting. Eric, wait for me in the classroom."

Eric wiped his nose on the back of his hand and glared at Cat. "This is your fault."

He threw her crumpled string as hard as he could. The light material landed on one of the low bleachers. Cat grabbed it before Mrs. Smith noticed.

Chapter 2 - The Worst Day

The teacher frowned at Cat. "Sit down where I told you. You're in double-detention. And you, Mr. Montgomery..." She wagged a finger at Peter. "I am very disappointed in you. You've always been such a well-behaved child. I'm writing your mother about this behavior."

He hung his head. "Yes, Mrs. Smith."

"You sit on the bleachers, too. On opposite ends! And no talking to each other!"

Cat's thread was in a terrible knot. She picked at it, head throbbing, as Mrs. Smith resumed her post watching the other kids. Peter sat on the far end of the bench as instructed and waved.

She mouthed the words "Thank you."

He gave a thumbs-up.

She pointed to his notebook and pantomimed drawing with an imaginary pencil on her hand.

He turned the notebook to show her. The drawing was little more than a blob of wiggly lines, but it was definitely going to be a new treasure map. She couldn't wait to get out of class so the two could try it out.

Chapter 3
Things you Can't Draw

Mrs. Smith figured out Cat copied her homework and assigned her a big research paper to make up the points. Cat's backpack was again full of books and worksheets. Peter carried what didn't fit in her backpack so she didn't have to use the pillow case again. He finished most of his homework in class, so he had extra room.

"Thanks for getting in trouble for me," Cat said. She pulled off her hat. "You were way

Chapter 3 - Things You Can't Draw

better protection than this dumb thing."

"What are best friends for?" Peter smiled.

"Will your mom be mad you got detention? Last time she flipped out about 'shaming your father's name' and junk."

"That was last year. She's calmed down a lot since then." Peter said. "Besides, when I tell her why it happened she'll be on our side."

Cat grinned. "You're right. She loves me."

"For better or worse," he teased and nodded to her dirty hat. "How's your bump?"

"It hurts. Dr. Charles says I have a something called a con-cushion."

"That's concussion," Peter said. "I think it means your brain is swollen."

"I believe it." Cat poked her bandage. The shapes scrambled around in the corners of her eyes. "Have you ever had one? A concussion?"

"I don't think so. Maybe."

"When you did, did you… see anything?"

Peter's brow leveled behind his glasses. "Are you seeing something?"

"Yeah...shapes."

"Shapes?"

Cat gulped. "I see them kind of floating around everywhere."

"That's probably a bad thing," Peter said.

"What do the shapes look like?"

"I don't know. Lines drawn with light."

"Are they letters like words?"

"No, just patterns. Like braids and knots."

Peter's brow furrowed deeper. "I don't understand what you mean."

"Like this..." Cat tried to trace one of the shapes with her finger as it floated past her eyes, but focusing on it only made it vanish.

Peter shook his head. "Maybe you should try drawing them on paper instead."

"I guess I can try that."

"If you draw them, I can look them up in

Chapter 3 - Things You Can't Draw

my dad's medical book. Then we can see what they are." Peter stopped in front of Cat's house and pulled her extra books out of his backpack. "Do you want to come over after dinner? We can look up the shapes and I can help you redo the homework you failed."

"That would be awesome," Cat said.

"I'll see you later, then." Peter smiled. "I'm glad you're feeling better."

"Kinda better."

"Kinda better's still better."

He headed next door and Cat hopped up the steps to her own house. Dad was home and helping Mom set the table for dinner. Dad smiled when he saw Cat. "Well? Did you survive your first day back?"

"Barely." Cat dropped her stack of books on the couch. "I got detention for not paying attention in class."

"Again?" Mom cried. "Cat, we talked about this. One more detention and you're grounded for a week."

Cat's face reddened. "Then I guess I shouldn't tell you I got detention a second time for fighting at recess."

"What? Fighting?" Mom cried. "Since when did you start getting in fights?"

19

"It wasn't my fault! Eric started it."

"I don't care who started it!"

"No, she's probably right." Dad said. "That Eric is a troublemaker. His father is a troublemaker, too. I'll speak to him about this."

"I don't care about Eric's father." Mom rubbed her eyes. "We'll talk about this later. Right now, let's eat dinner and Cat can tell us what she learned at school."

Cat sat down as mom pulled a whole roast out of the oven. "Wow!" Cat said. "Is it someone's birthday or something?"

Mom set the roast in the middle of the table. "No, but I thought it would be nice to celebrate the fact you're feeling better."

Cat blushed. "It's just a bumped head."

"It was worse than that." Dad sat down across from her. "You don't remember because of the bump, but we were really worried about you. Dr. Charles thought you'd hurt yourself badly. We're so excited that you've recovered without any problems."

The shapes in Cat's eyes swarmed around his smiling face. She swallowed hard and smiled back. "Yep, no problems at all."

The roast was delicious. Cat's family didn't eat meat very often. There wasn't room

Chapter 3 - Things You Can't Draw

to raise many animals in Mason Forge so anything fancier than a chicken had to be ordered from the big city and took at least two days to arrive. Cat had never been to the big city, or anywhere past the forest outside the town gate.

Dad cleared his throat and waited for Cat to stop shoveling food in her mouth. "So what did you learn in school today, Cat?"

She mixed a spoonful of peas in her mashed potatoes and took a big bite. "It's magic class time."

"Ugh." Dad rolled his eyes. "I think teaching that stuff to children is wrong."

"It's important kids learn the truth about the world," Mom said. "What if they go out and run into Curses? We should prepare them."

Cat's appetite vanished. Curses were the one part of magic class she remembered well. They were monsters disguised as normal people that caused bad things to happen. Kids had nightmares about Curses.

"See? That's the kind of stuff they want you to think," Dad said. "They say they know the truth, but they can say whatever they want and make the people believe it. We should be allowed to make up our own minds."

"Cat can already make up her own mind, can't you Cat?" Mom asked.

The shapes were on her food now, making even the roast look unappetizing. Cat poked her peas with her fork. "It was easier before I had a bump on my head."

Mom leaned forward and patted her wrist. "I'm sorry, honey. I know you don't like it when we argue. Dad was just talking about one of his crazy theories."

"It's not a theory if it's true," Dad said.

Dinner ended early, so after Cat moved the dirty dishes to the sink she got out her art supplies and sat at the table to try and draw some of the shapes for Peter. They were moving fast because she was still anxious after Mom and Dad's talk about Curses and Calligraphers.

Mom and Dad never agreed on political and religious stuff, mostly because of Dad who really didn't like magic in any form. Thinking about it made the shapes quiver, so Cat focused instead on drawing.

It was impossible to stare at any one shape for a length of time. Training both eyes on them made them shoot off or fade away. She tried to examine the ones hovering at the sides of her head in her peripheral vision. There were

Chapter 3 - Things You Can't Draw

a lot of circles and diamonds. Overlapping lines made spikey half-moons or stripes.

Cat copied the parts she noticed the most, filling the page with random lines as she rushed to mark each shape down. Patterns emerged. Every half-moon came with a diamond nearby, and linked squares would twirl to form snakes. Cat drew the bits she saw most often with different colors until the page was a rainbow of different shapes.

She held the page up to look at it all at once. The shapes in her eyes flew down to fit themselves to the pencil marks they most resembled, like individual pieces looking for the spot they belonged in a jigsaw puzzle.

"What are you doing over there, Cat?" Dad asked.

"Drawing."

"Can I see?" Dad leaned over her shoulder a moment. His smile vanished and with sudden anger, he snatched the paper from her hands and ripped it into pieces.

"Hey!" Cat was aghast. "That was mine!"

Dad stuffed the ripped pieces in his pockets. "Where did you see these symbols?"

She bit her lip, not sure how to explain it or if she even should. "Kind of everywhere?"

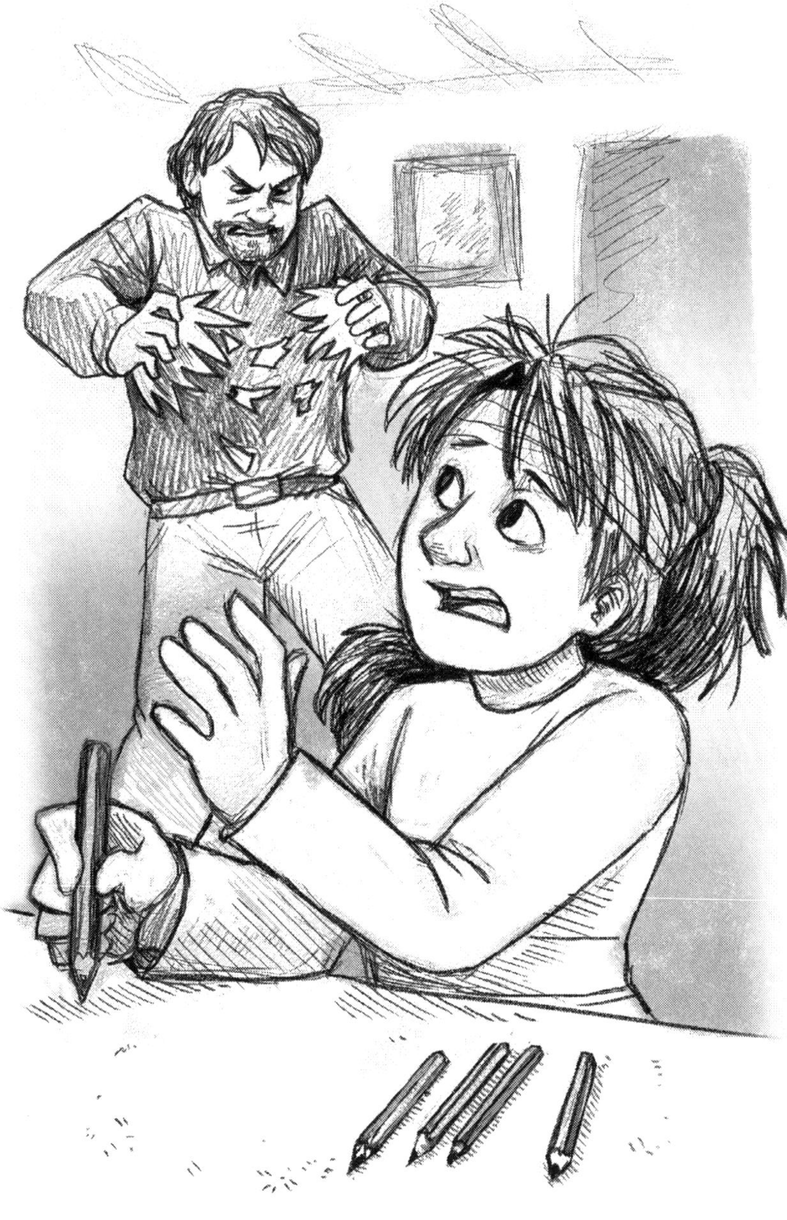

Chapter 3 - Things You Can't Draw

"I never want you to draw these symbols again, do you understand?" Dad said. "I want you to forget all about them."

"I would if I could!"

"Don't take that tone with me!"

Cat's head pounded. The shapes raced around her head in a whirlwind. She hated them! They ruined her homework. They put her in detention. Now they got her in trouble with Dad. She climbed onto the seat of the chair where she was sitting so that she and Dad were almost the same height and stomped her foot. "This isn't my fault!"

"That's it, young lady!" Dad shouted back. "Go to your room!"

"Fine! I'm grounded from too many detentions anyway!" Cat stomped up the hall and slammed her door shut. The sound of the slam made the shapes swarming around her head tremble.

Chapter 4
Sneaking Out

Cat sat and pouted in the middle of her bed all evening. She didn't even come out to get her homework, just played with her loop of string and waited until it was dark.

Mom knocked on her door. "Cat, honey, are you okay?"

"Hmph!" Cat replied.

"Your father and I talked." Mom's voice dipped sadly. "We are grounding you until the weekend. That's three days."

Chapter 4 - Sneaking Out

"Ugh," Cat groaned.

"If you're good, maybe we'll reconsider," Mom said. "We know you're still recovering, but fighting at school and now talking back to your dad. I don't know what's gotten in to you."

Cat hung her head. It was shapes. Shapes got into her. But she couldn't talk about it to Mom and Dad, not after what happened with the drawing.

A moment of silence passed. Mom spoke again. "It's time for bed."

"Yes, Mom."

"I love you."

Cat waited for Mom's footsteps to walk away. A door opened and closed deeper in the house. Cat hoped that meant her parents were going to sleep, too. She put on her shoes and turned off the lamp before climbing out her bedroom window and into the back yard.

The yard backed up to a forested patch that connected to the woods that separated Mason Forge from the rest of the world. Cat was careful not to leave footprints in the dirt as she jogged over the crusty grass to the side yard between her house and Peter's house. His window was near the front. Cat knocked on the glass until a light came on.

Peter opened the window, dressed in his pajamas. "You didn't come over for homework."

"I got sent to my room," Cat said.

"It's okay. Mom grounded me when she found out I got detention, so you couldn't have stayed anyway."

"I thought you said she wouldn't be mad at you because she loved me."

"Apparently she doesn't love you as much as I thought." Peter crossed his arms on the window sill. "I can't play outside for two days."

"I can't play for three." She beckoned. "Come out, let's do your treasure map."

Peter snorted. "And get in more trouble?"

"No one's going to find out," Cat said. "Besides, you can help me with my homework while we walk."

Peter adjusted his glasses. "I guess homework is a valuable reason to break rules."

"I knew you'd see it my way!"

Peter disappeared back into his room. The light went off and he climbed out the window, wearing his clothes from earlier. Peter pulled a folded bit of paper from his pocket. "The map's not done yet, but we can do what I have."

"Good. Let's go."

The two charged across the yard and

Chapter 4 - Sneaking Out

into the forest. When they were really little, Cat and Peter would explore the woods all day, pretending they were adventurers. Peter would trace the maps in his grandfather's atlas, or make them up from his imagination. Even though they never left the forest, they'd use the trees as landmarks and pretend they were in foreign places.

The actual forest stretched for miles down the mountain. It was too far for Cat to walk on her own, and she knew it ended at a desert that was even further to cross before they reached the big city. In daylight the woods were easy to navigate, but at night the trees were white as ghosts. Roots stuck out of the ground. Wind from the mountaintop creaked through the stiff branches, stirring curled brown leaves with the smell of turned dirt from the fields. Mom warned Cat not to wander far, but Cat and Peter knew the woods better than anyone.

Peter marked on his map with a pencil as they went. "I'm putting some cool places on this one, you're going to like it a lot. The treasure's going to be by the dry creek bed."

She slapped his arm. "Don't spoil it!"

"Sorry!" He laughed and scribbled on page. "So why did you get sent to your room?"

"Technically, it was for talking back, but it was really because of the shapes."

"The shapes in your head?"

"Yeah." Cat walked along an exposed root. "I was drawing them so I could show you, and Dad totally freaked out."

"So he knew what they were?"

"I guess."

"Did he tell you?"

"Heck no! He ripped the paper up and told me never to draw them again," Cat said. "I'm not asking him about it either. I'm in trouble enough as it is."

"Then maybe we should work on your homework," Peter said. "What are you going to write your research paper on?"

"I don't know. It has to be about magic."

"Then let's think of some topics," Peter said. "What was the question you got in trouble for not answering in class today?"

The shapes in her eyes clustered closer together as Cat replayed the events of the day. "How do Calligraphers do magic?"

"Do you know?"

Cat kicked a twig. "They paint it."

"They use calligraphy. Like their name."

"But that's like painting, right?"

Chapter 4 - Sneaking Out

"It's writing. With paint brushes."

"Paint-writing," Cat said.

"Sure." Peter tucked his map in his pocket and jumped to catch a hanging branch. The limb creaked as he pulled himself into the tree. "They paint on the ground and make magic."

"Like fireballs?"

"And wind and boulders and stuff." Peter climbed to a higher branch. "The Calligraphers use runes. Runes are magic symbols."

"Symbols?"

"Shapes."

"Shapes..." Cat blinked. The dry branches of the old tree crisscrossed to resemble the patterns in her drawings. She traced their lines with her eyes, grabbed a lower branch, and followed Peter up the tree. "I don't want to write my paper about that."

"Okay, there are other topics you can pick," Peter said. "What about the Curses, we'll be learning about them next."

"I don't want to write about Curses. Curses are scary." Cat climbed higher.

"They're not scary like you think they are," Peter said. "They're just a different type of magic. Bad magic instead of the Calligraphers' good magic. They mostly cause bad luck."

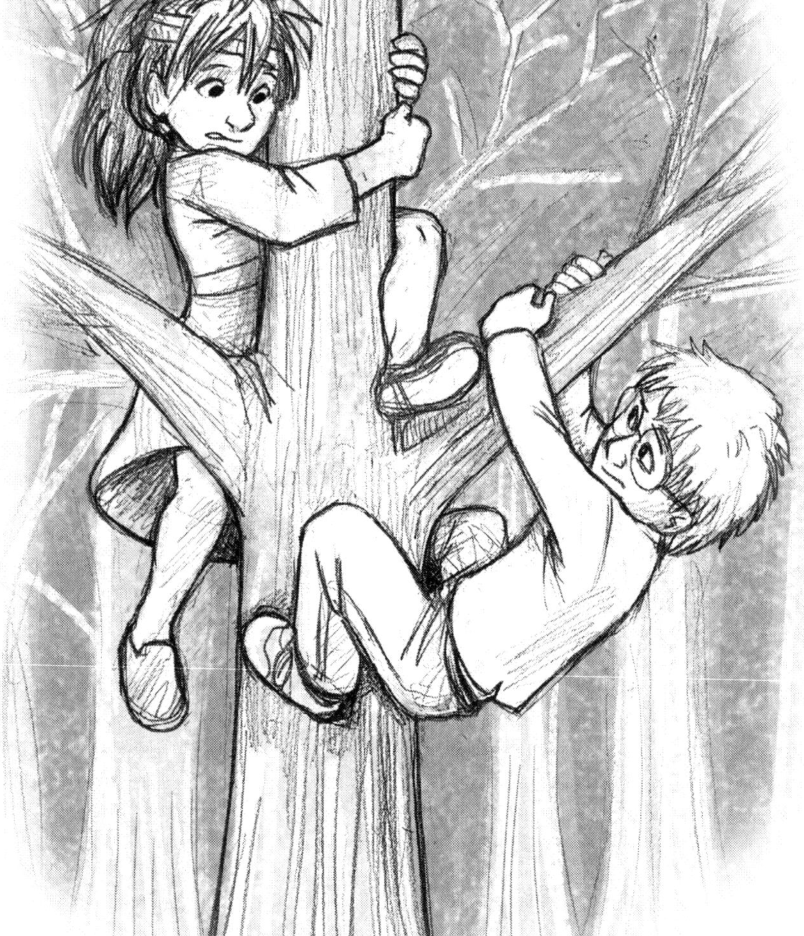

Chapter 4 - Sneaking Out

"Bad luck isn't so bad."

"And since you'll be taking notes on Mrs. Smith's talk tomorrow anyway, you can do your essay homework at the same time. Just turn the notes into your paper."

"Ooh! Clever!" Cat grinned. "This is why you're the smartest kid in town."

"D'aw." Peter sat on the highest branch. "You just said that because I'm your favorite."

"You're my favorite because you're you. Being smart is an extra."

The tree they sat in shuddered. Something cracked. A jagged split opened on the branch where Peter was sitting.

"Pete! Look out!"

The branch broke and dropped Peter from the tree. He bounced off a lower limb and landed in the dirt. Cat's heart pounded as she scrambled down. The shapes swirled like a whirlwind and clouded her vision. "You okay?"

"Ow." Peter sat up. "My ankle hurts."

"Did you break it?"

"No, I can still move it. That means it's not broken." He reached for her. "Help me up."

Cat pulled him back to his feet, but he winced when he stepped down. His ankle was already swelling up.

"This is bad," Cat said. "We're both supposed to be grounded. We are going to get in real trouble when our parents find out."

"It's not like I can pretend it didn't happen." He tried to step down again and winced. "Can you help me walk?"

Cat wrapped her arm around his back and helped him toward the house. The shapes waved back and forth like a path in front of her. She didn't care about getting in trouble. This was her fault. She was the one who broke the rules and sneaked out. Peter even said 'no' but she begged him to come. He was helping her and got hurt. Guilt felt like a stone weighing down her stomach.

Chapter 4 - Sneaking Out

Cat got them back to the side-yard between their houses. Peter reached for the open window, but Cat yanked him away.

"What are you doing?" Peter asked.

"Let me handle this," Cat said.

She knocked on the door. Peter's mom, Mrs. Montgomery, opened the door with Peter's little brother Alan on her hip.

"Peter what are you doing out here?" she asked. "I said you were grounded."

"Don't be mad at him, Mrs. Montgomery," Cat said. "He was helping me with my homework and hurt his ankle."

She raised one eyebrow. "How did he hurt his ankle helping with your homework?"

"We were doing it in a tree," Peter said.

Mrs. Montgomery rolled her eyes and boosted Alan in her arms. "I don't know what to do with you kids. Okay Peter, let's get you fixed up. Cat, go home. I'll talk to your mother about this in the morning."

Cat nodded. "Yes, ma'am."

Peter limped up the steps. Cat mouthed the word "sorry."

Peter mouthed back "it's okay" before the door shut beween them.

Chapter 5
Grounded

Cat dragged her pillowcase through the street, grumbling under her breath. Mom had lectured her for an hour about how disappointed she was, and made her late. The talk ended in Cat being grounded for an extra week. Her head was pounding less than before, but the shapes were still spinning.

Peter was already at his desk when she walked in. His right foot was wrapped from toes to shin in bandages. "Look, Cat. My foot and your head are twins."

Chapter 5 - Grounded

She forced a laugh. "How bad is it?"

"My foot or how my mom reacted?"

"Both, I guess."

"Mom says my ankle's twisted. It'll be better in a couple days. And she was impressed with your confession of guilt. I guess she loves you after all."

"Does that mean you're not grounded?"

"Oh, I'm still grounded," he said. "Just not grounded more than I already was."

"Sit down everyone!" Mrs. Smith called. "We have a guest speaker today so be extra well-behaved. I'm looking at you, Catrina."

Cat sank deeper into her seat.

Mrs. Smith knocked on the door to the office behind her desk and an old man with a bald head and thick glasses came out. It was Dr. Charles, the man who diagnosed Cat's concussion. Seeing him made her thoughts swim, like she'd forgotten something important. The shapes swirled in front of her eyes, but she waved them away and got out a clean piece of paper to take notes for her essay.

"Hello kids, how are you all doing today?" Dr. Charles asked. The class murmured in reply. Dr. Charles wrote his name on the chalkboard. "I already know all of you, and I know you all

37

know me, but do you know why I'm here to talk to you today?"

Jenny, Eric's bossy friend, raised her hand. "Health class?"

Dr. Charles laughed with a soft grunt. "Sort of, I suppose. Mrs. Smith asked me here because you've been learning about magic this week and there's a very important part of magic studies you have yet to cover. Tell me, kids, who is the oldest?"

A dark-skinned boy named Bobby raised his hand. "I'm ten!"

"Good. And who is the youngest?"

Brett's little sister Patty spoke up. "I'm four years old."

"That's perfect," Dr. Charles said. "Today we are talking about Curses. Curses are bad magic. They're a punishment for all the bad things people do."

Patty interrupted him. "Brett says there are Curses hiding in my closet that will eat me."

Brett, Eric, and Jenny snickered. Mrs. Smith clicked her tongue to shush them.

"I doubt there are Curses in your closet and they certainly will not eat you," Dr. Charles said. "But your brother is right that Curses could be anywhere. They are born to human

Chapter 5 - Grounded

parents and grow up like normal kids, but they are actually evil creatures in disguise."

Patty gulped. "Creatures?"

"Curses start out looking normal, but from the moment they are born they are transforming into misshapen monsters made of magical elements like fire, water, wind, and rock. By the time a Curse grows up, it will no longer look human at all, having been fully changed into the creature. Curses are more than just frightening to look at. Their presence causes natural disasters and bad luck to anyone nearby. And they could be anyone."

Cat gulped. The shapes in her eyes crowded Dr. Charles's face. Dad said the shapes were bad. Peter said the Calligraphers used symbols to cast magic. Was it bad magic?

Eric spoke, sounding less confident than usual. "Does that mean one could be here?"

"It's possible," Dr. Charles said. "Most Curses start to show signs at about your age."

"My age?" Patty asked.

"Yes. Any one of you could be a Curse."

The students started exchanging suspicious glances as if their friends were secretly monsters. Cat's heart pounded in her chest. Ever since she bumped her head she'd been in trouble: from the fight on the playground, to the drawing, to Peter's twisted ankle. The shapes whirled about in blurry circles. She raised her hand. "Dr. Charles?"

Mrs. Smith frowned, but the doctor pointed to her. "Yes, Catrina?"

"How – " Cat's voice was shaky. She cleared her throat. "How do you know if you are a Curse or not?"

"That's hard to answer. There are symptoms, but they are different for every Curse," Dr. Charles said.

She swallowed hard. "What will happen to us if we end up being a Curse?"

"The Holy Calligraphers made laws long ago about how to deal with Curses," Dr. Charles said. "It is dangerous for Curses to live with normal people because of the misfortune they cause, so the Calligraphers have built places out in the desert for the Curses to live. Any children who are discovered to be Curses must go there."

Cat felt sick. She didn't want to turn into a monster or be forced to live in the desert away from Peter and her parents.

Her nerves must have registered on her face. Dr. Charles softened his voice into the

Chapter 5 - Grounded

consoling tone he used when she was sick. "Don't worry Catrina, there hasn't been a Curse in Mason Forge for over one-hundred years. There's a very slim chance one is hiding among your classmates."

Dr. Charles raised his voice again and spoke to the whole class. "This is why I'm here. Only a doctor can determine if you are showing signs of being a Curse. I will see each of you one at a time for a special check-up to make sure everybody is who they are supposed to be, so no one needs to be scared."

Dr. Charles started with the front row. Mrs. Smith took her place at the chalkboard and repeated what the doctor said so the kids could write it down. Cold sweat soaked the back of Cat's shirt. Hands shaking, she tried to take notes but her heart was rattling. The shapes in her head were shaking too. Everything from her brains to her bones trembled in fear as she waited her turn.

"Catrina Aston?" Dr. Charles called.

Cat jumped. The doctor beckoned her into the teacher's office as Eric returned to his seat, looking relieved.

Cat's knees shook so much she had to lean on her desk to stand up. She stared over her shoulder at Peter. His brow was pinched tight, but he gave her a smile and nodded like it was going to be okay. Cat took a deep breath of cool air to settle her stomach and hurried to the teacher's office. Dr. Charles closed the door, sealing the two of them inside.

"Hello, Catrina. How are you feeling today?" Dr. Charles asked.

"Fine." Cat said, too quickly.

Dr. Charles paused. "How's that bump?"

"It's good," she said. The shapes spun past her eyes at top speed, like she was caught in a whirlwind of knots and circles. "There's nothing weird going on!"

Chapter 5 - Grounded

Dr. Charles frowned. "Is there anything you want me to know about?"

"Nope! Nothing!"

Dr. Charles glanced down at her wiggling knees. She clenched her muscles to keep them from knocking. The doctor gave a low "hmm" and wiped a thermometer with a disinfectant cloth. "Open wide."

She did.

He stuck it in her mouth. "Have you had any swelling anywhere? Wrists? Ankles?"

Cat shook her head "no" and the shapes swirled around like stirred cereal.

"Lots of sweating?"

A bead of sweat ran down the side of her face, but she shook her head "no" again.

"Difficulty catching your breath?" Dr. Charles took the thermometer out of Cat's mouth to check her temperature.

Cat swallowed hard and blinked fast to scatter the shapes again. "No, sir. I'm totally one-hundred percent normal. Promise."

"But you are hiding something." Dr. Charles leaned on his elbow. "Do you have something you want to tell me?"

Cat gulped.

"Did my talk before scare you?"

"A little?"

"Well, you don't have to worry, everything about you is perfectly normal," Dr. Charles said. "You can go back to your seat now."

Cat gnawed her lip and hurried out of the office like she'd stolen something.

Peter watched her, expectantly. Cat gave him a thumbs up, but her hand still trembled.

"Mr. Montgomery?" Dr. Charles called.

Peter limped into the teacher's office. Cat opened her notebook and tried to catch up on the part of Mrs. Smith's lesson she missed during her checkup. They were learning more about the Curse Towns and how the Calligraphers forced the healthy people nearby to feed the Curses even though they were dangerous. Cat's hand shook as she scribbled through the storm of dancing shapes and knots. It wasn't until the lesson ended that she noticed Peter wasn't back from the office.

"Alright everyone. Pull out your math books," Mrs. Smith said. Cat pulled her book out of her backpack and did a page full of problems. Peter still wasn't back.

More time passed. Mrs. Smith erased her example problems off the blackboard. "Okay, time for recess. Anyone who hasn't had Dr.

Chapter 5 - Grounded

Charles's checkup will have one after lunch."

"Um, excuse me?" Cat raised her hand.

Mrs. Smith pointed. "Yes, Catrina?"

"Is Peter – "

"He'll join us outside when he's done," she said. "Everyone out."

The other kids rushed into the yard, overflowing with nervous energy after such a stressful lesson. Patty and the youngest kids started a game of tag. The older kids joined as they were tagged by the different "its."

Cat was too worried to play. She pulled her loop of string off her wrist and started twisting patterns. The games she'd memorized didn't help like they usually did. The floating shapes in her eyes vibrated so fast they were a blur. Cat twisted and traded loops at random. The shapes snapped to the string when the crisscross pattern happened to resemble them.

Cat pulled her hands free of the string and gave up trying to sooth herself. There was nothing she could do to calm down except find out what happened to Peter.

Mrs. Smith watched the tag game with interest. Cat waited until her back was turned and sneaked around the school house to a place where she was safely hidden from sight.

The teacher's office had a window halfway up the back wall. Cat rose to her tiptoes, but still wasn't tall enough to see inside the office. The brick wall below the window had a lot of ridges and broken bits, but none of the hand or foot holds were strong enough to climb on.

Cat searched the back of the school for a ladder or something to stand on. The grass was curled and dry with lots of rocks, but nothing big enough to use as a step. She could drag over a bench from the playground, but something that large was hard to move and Mrs. Smith would catch her. The shapes flitted around until she spotted a metal trash can where the tangles settled like a target.

"You belong in the trash, you stupid shapes," Cat muttered. As soon as Mrs. Smith was distracted, Cat grabbed the trash can and dragged it to the space below the window.

Cat pressed herself flat to the brick, listening for a shout from someone who saw her, or for Mrs. Smith to appear around the corner and catch her, but no one came. Cat took a couple breaths and turned the can over, dumping the half-eaten lunches and wadded napkins into a pile. She climbed up onto the upside-down can and peered into the teacher's

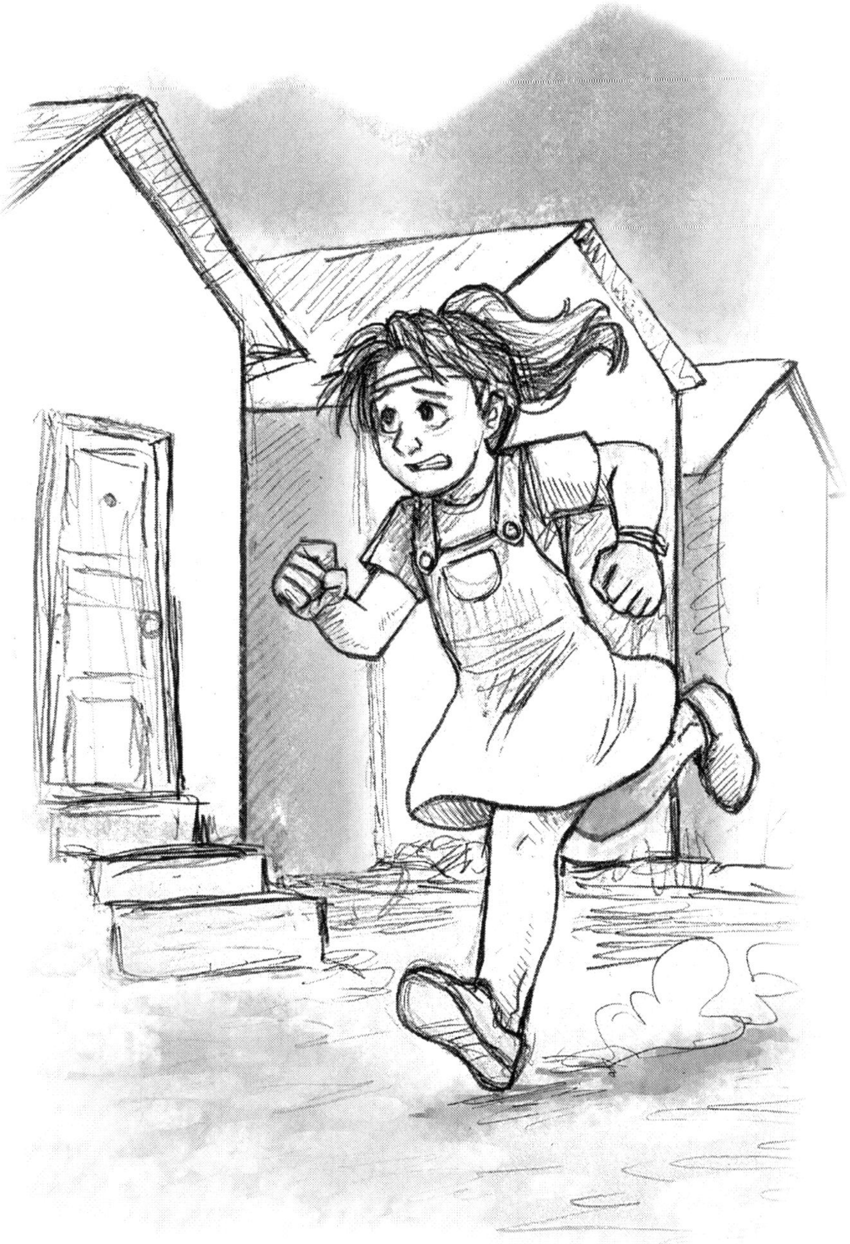

office through the window.

The door was open and the room was empty. Peter and Dr. Charles were gone.

The twist in Cat's stomach made her want to throw up. Shapes swarmed her vision. She swiped her arms to try and clear them, but they wouldn't go away. They flashed white with each pulse of her heartbeat.

Cat didn't care if Mrs. Smith saw her, she had to get to Peter's house. If she was wrong, he wouldn't be there and she'd get in trouble for skipping class, but if she was right….

Cat jumped down from the trash can and ran across the playground. Mrs. Smith shouted, but Cat didn't stop. The shapes grew thick enough to block her view of the road, but she focused hard and they dispersed, leaving the path ahead clear as she sprinted at top speed. Peter's mom was crying loud enough to hear it in the street. Cat opened Peter's front door. Mom and Dad were there with Dr. Charles. Mrs. Montgomery cradled Alan as she sobbed, but Peter was still missing.

Dr. Charles spoke, his face sad. "Catrina."

"Peter," she panted. "He's a Curse, right?"

Dr. Charles looked away. "Yes, he is."

Chapter 6
The New Worst Day

Cat sat on a hard stool, too upset to speak. Her father held her shoulders from behind, as if he was afraid she was going to run away. She tugged the loop of string on her wrist, but her fingers felt numb. The floating shapes twirled in circles when she blinked, but she was so sad and angry she barely noticed they were there.

Mom held Mrs. Montgomery while she cried. Dad spoke to Dr. Charles. "Are you certain he's a Curse?"

"Positive," Dr. Charles said. "It was his twisted ankle that proved it. It's normal for an ankle to swell, but Peter's ankle had a hard knot in it. When I looked closer, I found more growing in his feet and hands. These are the first symptoms of being an Earth Curse."

"What does that mean?" Mom asked.

"It means he's turning to stone," Dr. Charles said. "He will have to go to the desert to live with other Earth Curses like him."

Cat swallowed hard. Her voice was choked when she spoke. "He'll go there to get better?"

"No," said Dr. Charles. "This isn't the kind of sickness someone gets better from."

Mrs. Montgomery sobbed harder. Mom hugged her and told her it was going to be all right. Anger boiled in Cat's chest. Mom was lying. It wasn't going to be all right at all. Thick tears filled Cat's eyes. "It isn't fair."

"I know, but that's how life is sometimes," Dr. Charles said.

"You have to do something to fix him."

"I would if I could. Please believe me." Dr. Charles knelt down in front of her and tried to sound positive. "I know it's hard to accept, but sometimes bad things happen."

Chapter 6 - The New Worst Day

"That's not good enough." Cat gave him her meanest look. "Peter's not a monster."

"He doesn't look like it, but he is."

"No he's not!" Cat stood up so fast she knocked the stool over. Dad's hands came off her shoulders as he stepped out of the way.

Mom frowned at her. "Cat, don't yell."

"I want to yell!" Cat said. "Everyone needs to know this isn't fair! Peter didn't do anything wrong. He's the nicest person in the world!"

"That may be true, but getting sick can

happen to anyone, it doesn't matter how nice they are." Dr. Charles said. "Being sick can happen to anyone. As a doctor, I would know."

"I don't want to hear you talk anymore," Cat snapped at him. "If you can't help Peter, then you're no good to anyone! You're awful. I wish you were the Curse instead!"

"Catrina!" Mom shouted.

Cat didn't want to get in more trouble. She ran out the front door and into the side yard between Peter's house and hers. No one followed her, so Cat leaned on the wall and started crying. The shapes rippled in her teary eyes like the surface of a pond.

She heard someone else crying, too. The sound was coming from Peter's bedroom window. Cat didn't bother knocking this time, she pushed open the window and climbed in.

Peter was sitting on his bed with his bandaged foot on a pillow. His eyes were bright red with tears dripping down his chin. Cat hugged him around the neck so tight his glasses dug into her shoulder. Peter hugged her back, sniffing and swallowing. She wished she could make him feel better, but there was nothing she could do. His body was still sick.

"You're not a monster," Cat said. "They

Chapter 6 - The New Worst Day

can't make you leave if you don't want to."

"I don't think they care," Peter said.

Cat hugged tighter. "Then I'll stop them."

"How?"

"I don't know, but I won't let them take you away."

She looked around his room. The shapes floated in circles, fitting themselves to the square pictures, round balls, and zig-zag corners around the room. They drifted until they found Peter's unfinished treasure map open on his desk and settled themselves to the lines and mountains.

"The shapes."

"What?"

"The map!" Cat jumped off the bed. "My shapes are pointing to your map. Maybe they're telling us we need to run away."

"Run away?" Peter's teary eyes widened. "We can't do that!"

"Why not?"

"Where will we go?"

"Anywhere." The shapes scattered as Cat snatched the treasure map off Peter's desk. "No one knows the woods better than we do. We can build a tent somewhere. Live off the land like real adventurers. If the grown-ups can't

53

find you, they can't send you away."

He bit his lip. "I guess."

"So what do you say?"

Peter frowned at his bandaged foot, thinking hard. Cat fidgeted with the string on her wrist as she waited. He took a deep breath and put his bandaged foot carefully on the floor. "Okay. Let's go."

Cat dumped his school bag on the floor, stepping on papers as she filled the bag with Peter's clothes and a bunch of granola bars he kept in his desk for adventures. She put the bag on her back and climbed out of his window.

Peter put his twisted ankle out the window and lowered himself into Cat's waiting arms. She made sure he landed softly and put his arm around her shoulders to help him walk through the yard and to the woods.

The roots and logs seemed more dangerous with Peter limping beside her. She guided him carefully over each one.

He stumbled and grabbed her shoulders tightly. "Watch out!"

"It's okay, I've got you."

"I can't fall," he said. "Dr. Charles told me. My bones are weak. They'll break if I fall again."

"I won't let you fall," Cat said.

Chapter 6 - The New Worst Day

He gulped. "You promise?"

She nodded. "I will never let you fall."

The two continued through the afternoon. Cat picked open areas to walk, but avoided the main road in case the adults were following them. Before long, it started to get dark.

Cat paused by a tree trunk. Peter leaned on it, sweat soaking his shirt. He looked pale. Cat touched his arm. "Does it hurt?"

He took a deep breath and nodded.

"Maybe you should sit down."

Cat held onto his shoulders and lowered him to the dirt between two exposed roots. Peter slouched against the tree and rubbed his eyes with the heels of his hands.

Cat sat down nearby. "You okay?"

"No," he muttered with a sob in his voice. "I can't believe this has happened."

Cat released all the breath from her lungs. Part of her still hoped the doctor was wrong.

"What's going to happen to you if I turn into a monster while we're out here together?" His glasses fogged up. "What happens if something bad happens to you?"

"It doesn't matter," Cat said. "You'll never be a monster to me. You're you. That's the most important part."

He nodded, but the look on his face was far from calm. Cat pulled the loop of string off her wrist and stretched it between her hands. She made the first step of the two-player Child's Cradle game and held it toward him.

"Your turn."

Peter scoffed. "I don't want to play."

"Come on, it'll get your mind off things." She nudged the string forward. "It helps me. Give it a try."

Peter sighed again and reached up to pinch the 'x's formed by the crossing strings. He twisted his wrists and removed the cradle shape to make a diamond pattern between his own hands. Cat reached in and grabbed two more 'x's to take the string back, changing the pattern into stripes.

"You know, these remind me of my shapes," she said.

"The ones you see in air?" Peter hooked his fingers in the stripes and transferred the string back to his hands and made the diamonds again.

"Yeah they overlap like these do." Cat pinched the strings and took the thread back. The new shape made a circle. She offered it back to him.

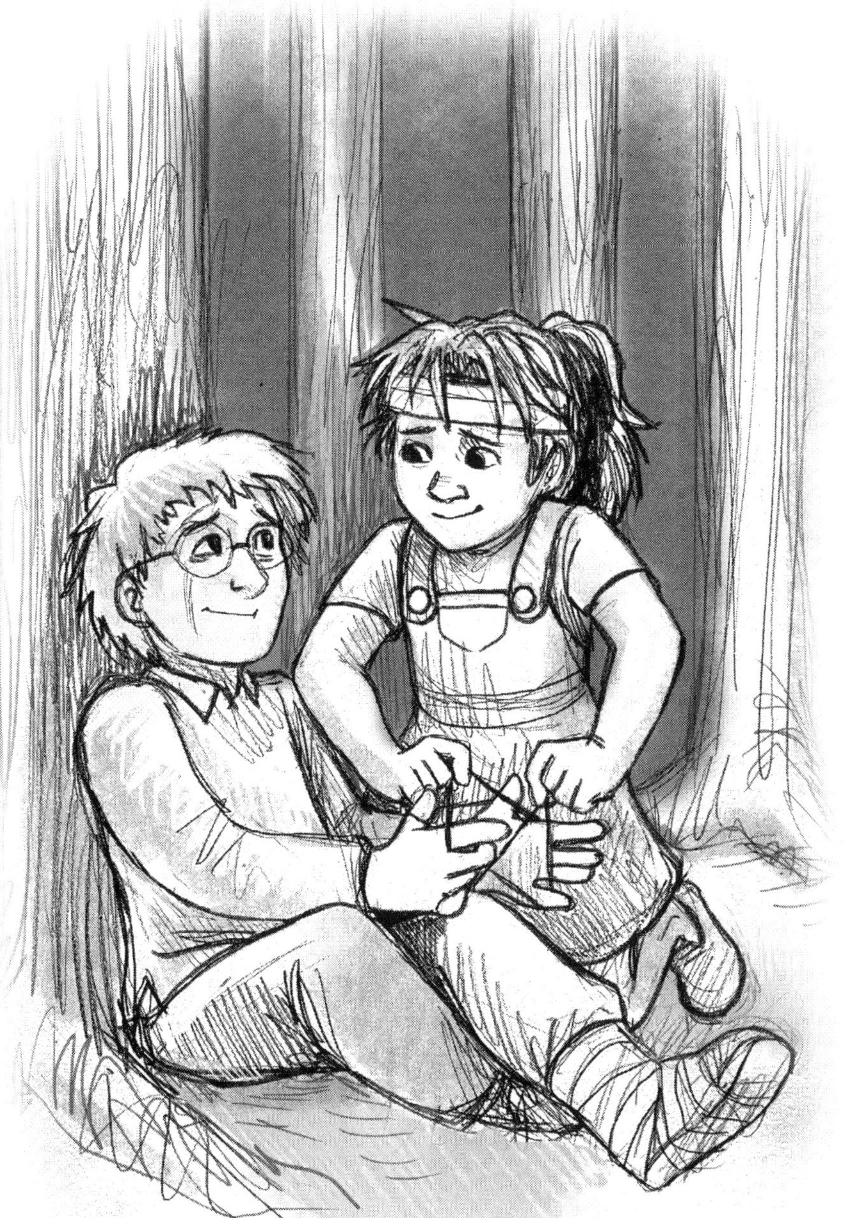

He pulled a couple loops to transfer them to his hands. "Can you see them right now?"

"Yeah, but they're fainter." Cat tried to focus on a shape. It held still long enough for her to trace the line with her finger. "They were a lot brighter earlier when I thought you were in trouble."

Peter offered the string back to her. "What do you think they mean?"

"I'm not sure. I thought they meant something was wrong with me, but now I'm wondering if they're here for a reason." Cat took the string off his hands with a twist of her wrists and ended up back at the Child's Cradle shape again. "Do you feel any better?"

"Yeah, the string helped." He smiled faintly. "You're really smart, Cat."

She grinned. "You're just saying that because I'm your favorite."

"My absolute favorite," Peter said. "Thanks for staying my friend."

"You don't have to thank me," Cat said. "I'd rather be your friend than anything else."

Chapter 7
Escape!

Cat didn't realized she'd fallen asleep on Peter's shoulder until she heard her Mom's voice echoing off the white trees.

"Cat!"

"Pete, wake up." Cat whispered.

Peter rubbed his eye under his glasses. "When did it get dark?"

"Hush," she warned.

Her dad's voice came next. "Cat! Where are you? Answer us!"

"We have to run for it," Cat said.

Peter's brow knit. "I don't think I can."

"Then we'll walk for it." She pulled him up. He kept his weight off his bandaged ankle, but he was less pale and exhausted than before. Cat wound her arm around his back.

They took off through the woods again, dodging the white trunks. Branches reached like ghosts. Cat kept her eye on the ground, but the shapes in her vision kept floating in the way. She blinked extra fast to clear them. Peter stumbled, but Cat kept her arm around him and shuffled him through the trees.

"Cat!" Mom called again. She was closer this time. "Peter!"

Cat couldn't let them find him. If they caught up, Peter would be sent to the Curse Town for Earth Curses, and she would never see him again. He panted in her ear and moved as fast as he could on one leg.

"Cat!" Dad sounded angry now. His lantern shone through the trees in stripes. The lines in her vision slotted into place along the glowing beams.

They needed somewhere for Peter to hide. Cat stopped by a large tree and reached into their travel bag.

Chapter 7 - Escape!

Peter wheezed. "What are you doing?"

"Your treasure map." She pulled it out. "We need a place they can't find us."

"The treasure is in the dry creek bed." He pointed to a pencil mark along the north cliff. "There's a big boulder by the wall. We could hide there."

"Which way?"

He pointed behind them and to the left.

Cat held the map in one hand and Peter in the other. Going uphill was much harder than going downhill as they had been doing. Peter hopped on his good foot, capable of only toe-taps with his bad one. Cat pulled him along with her, but he was heavy and she wasn't used to carrying so much weight for so long.

Dad's lantern swept closer. "I think I saw something!"

Peter pinched her side. "Stop."

The two pressed close to a big tree. The lantern light spread across the ground on either side, barely missing them in the shadow of the pale trunk.

"Over here!" Mom called.

The lantern swept away and Cat hustled Peter forward. A steep rock face rose from the ground at the edge of the forest leading up to a mountain top high above the town. The boulder Peter mentioned stood out from the cliff, reflecting moonlight like a beacon. She adjusted her grip on him. "Hold on, we're almost there."

The ground dipped down at the edge of the trees, easing them into the dry creek bed. Dad's lantern swept through the forest further down the hill.

"Cat!" Mom shouted. She sounded like she was about to cry. "Cat, please answer!"

"You should go back," Peter panted.

"No way."

"But they're worried about you."

"I don't care."

Cat steered Peter into the moonlight and crouched with him behind the large boulder. Trembling, he sucked air with a grating sound, completely exhausted from the climb.

Cat knelt at the edge of the rock and watched the lantern move through the trees. "I think we're safe here."

"They sound really upset," Peter said. He flinched and grabbed at his un-bandaged leg.

"What's wrong?"

"My knee." He frowned. "And my foot. And my shin… it aches all over."

Chapter 7 - Escape!

"Maybe I can rub it." Cat squeezed Peter's knee through his pant leg.

He winced again. "No, don't."

"But..."

"It's going away on its own." He rested his head on the rock wall behind him. "It just needs to rest."

Cat's stomach did flips as she returned to his side. Mom and Dad were still calling for her further down the hill. They moved so fast compared to Peter, but at least they were walking away. She pulled out Peter's map.

The dry river was on the north side of the forest pass close to town. Cat's shoulders slouched. After walking all afternoon and running like crazy through the woods, they were not even a mile away from home.

Peter must have read the look on her face. "I told you we couldn't go fast."

All the sadness and exhaustion in her welled up as tears in her eyes. "I'm sorry."

"What are you sorry for?"

"I failed."

"You got us this far."

"I barely got us anywhere," she said. "Do you think Mom and Dad will give up looking for us and go home?"

He swallowed. "Would you give up?"

"No," she said.

"So what do we do now?"

She nestled in next to him. "Wait for them to find us. See how grounded we get."

"More grounded than we've ever been in our lives."

"Yeah, probably." Cat watched the shapes move. Two collided into a third shape that spiraled out of her view. "Can I ask you something?"

"Sure."

Chapter 7 - Escape!

"Did you really think my shapes were going to guide us somewhere when you agreed to run away?"

He paused. "I could tell you believed it."

"And that's all?"

"I can't see your shapes Cat, but I can definitely see you. You believed in them, and I believe in you, so I trusted you."

She sank further into his shoulder, feeling sad and weak. "Do you trust me less now that I let you down?"

"No." His voice was calm and his breathing was less wheezy. "Are you giving up?"

"I don't want to."

"I don't want to either," he said. "Maybe instead of trying something we can't do, we should think of something we can do."

Cat tugged at the string on her wrist, watching the shapes move in arcs on the rocks around her. The symbols shook like a ringing bell as Mom's voice echoed around her.

"Cat! Please come home!"

Mom was crying, it made Cat's name sound like a cough in her throat. Cat recognized how it felt, she'd had the same feeling on the playground when she didn't know what happened to Peter. Cat rose from

Peter's shoulder and motioned for him to stay put. "I have an idea."

"Cat!" Dad's lantern swept the woods a few yards downhill.

Cat stepped out into the dry riverbed and raised her arms. "Over here!"

The lantern flashed back toward her, blinding her as it caught her in its beam. She shielded her eyes as her father raced through the woods toward her. Mom skidded into the riverbed ahead of him with her face striped in tears and sweat. She reached for her daughter.

Cat threw up her hands. "Stop!"

To her surprise, Mom and Dad obeyed her. They stared at her like they couldn't believe she was really there.

Dad scanned the surrounding forest with his lamp. "Where's Peter?"

"I'm not going to let you have him if you're going to send him away," Cat said.

"Honey," Dad said firmly. "The law tells us what we have to do."

"I don't care." Cat said. "I want Peter to stay with me. You know he's good. Help him stay, or we're going to run away forever."

"Cat!" Mom cried.

"Please, Mom." Tears welled in her eyes.

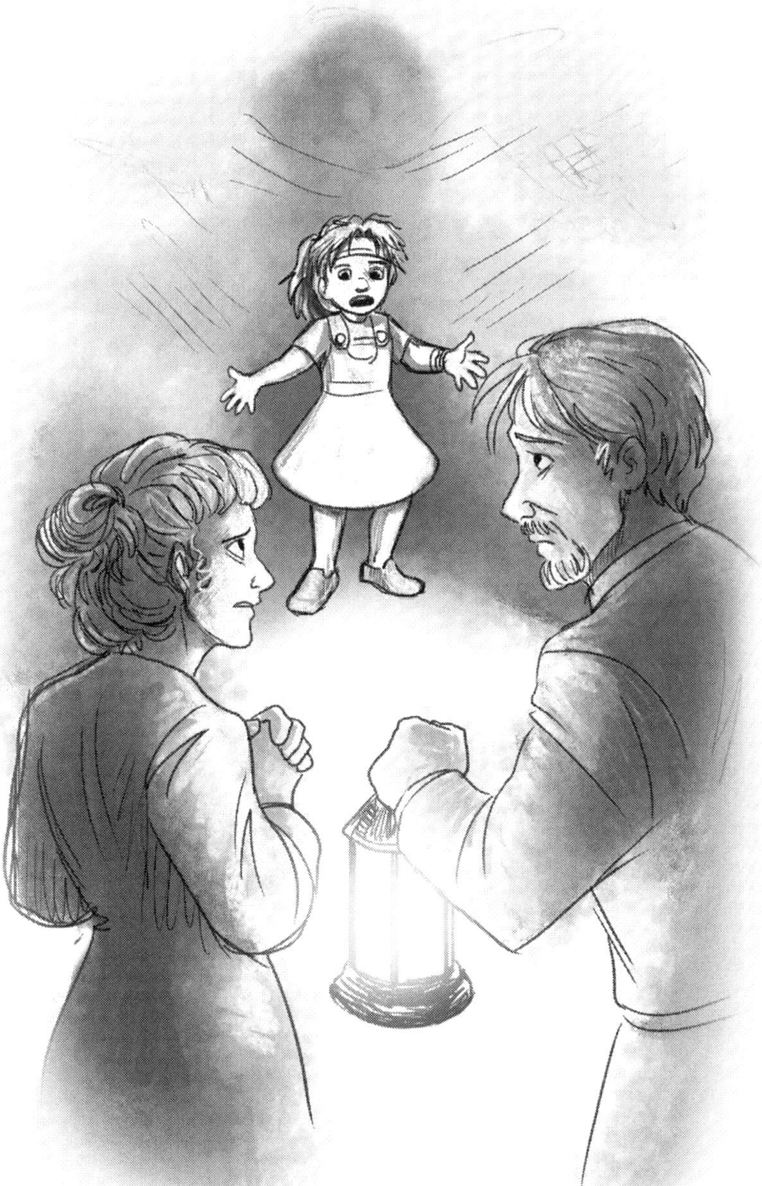

Mom's arms dropped to her sides. She looked to Dad. Cat couldn't see their faces because of the blinding light of the lantern. She held her breath until Dad spoke again.

"Okay," he said. "We'll figure something out, but you need to come home – "

"You promise?" Cat said. "I won't tell you unless you promise you'll help him stay."

"I promise," Dad said. He was using his serious voice. "Now where is he?"

Cat gestured to the rock behind her. "Right here."

Dad gave Mom the lantern and walked up to Peter. The shapes in Cat's eyes jittered, but faded as Dad reached out and took Peter's shoulder. "This has been a tough day, hasn't it?"

Peter swallowed. "Yes, sir."

"Your mom is really worried," Dad said. "Did you hurt yourself?"

"No, sir. I'm just tired."

"Okay, come here."

Dad let Peter hug him around the neck and lifted the boy off the ground in both arms. Cat took Mom's hand and the four of them began the slow, sad walk home.

Chapter 8
A New Plan

When they opened the door to Peter's house, Mrs. Montgomery's eyes were so heavy and red Cat barely recognized her.

"Peter!" The weeping woman nearly screamed as she grabbed her son from Dad's arms. "Where were you? I was so scared."

"Sorry, Mom," Peter mumbled.

"I'm sorry, Mrs. Montgomery," Cat said. "I made him run away so Dr. Charles couldn't make him leave."

Dr. Charles was in the living room. He cleared his throat. "It's not what I want to do, Catrina. It's the law."

Mrs. Montgomery rounded on him, her tear-stained face full of rage. "Get out!"

Mom let go of Cat's hand to reach for Mrs. Montgomery's shoulders. "Sheila, calm down."

"I said, go!" Mrs. Montgomery lurched back to get Peter out of Mom's reach.

Mom gasped. "I wasn't going to hurt him."

"Come on, dear," Dad said. He ushered Cat, Mom, and Dr. Charles out ahead of him.

Cat looked back as the door closed and saw Mrs. Montgomery sit down on the couch, hugging Peter tight.

Cat, her parents, and Dr. Charles moved to Cat's house next door. Mom had fresh tears in her eyes as she seated Cat at the kitchen table and went to make tea.

Cat didn't blame Mom for being upset. Just like Peter was Cat's best friend, Peter's mom was Mom's best friend, and it was hard to see someone she loved so upset. Mom wiped her eyes with a napkin and petted Cat's hair. Every time her fingers touched Cat's bump, the shapes in her eyes swirled.

Chapter 8 - A New Plan

"This has become more serious," Dr. Charles said to Dad. "Mrs. Montgomery is unable to make clear decisions. We need to act in her stead."

Dad's brow knit in a serious look. "What do you mean?"

"We must get the Curse out of town."

Cat's throat tightened. She stared at Dad's back, praying he remembered his promise.

Dad faced the doctor. "Let's not do anything rash."

"The boy is dangerous," Dr. Charles said. "You know this as well as I do."

"I know it even better than you do," Dad said. "Identifying the symptoms of a Curse is your job as a doctor, but I'm a lawyer and I know the laws."

"Exactly," Dr. Charles said. "That's why we must send the child to Earth Town if his mother cannot. It's the law the Calligraphers made regarding Curses."

"And laws are enforced by the mayor, not you and me," Dad said. "Peter will be just as much of a Curse tomorrow as he is today. We need to consider our options and what is best for the boy."

"What is best for the boy doesn't matter

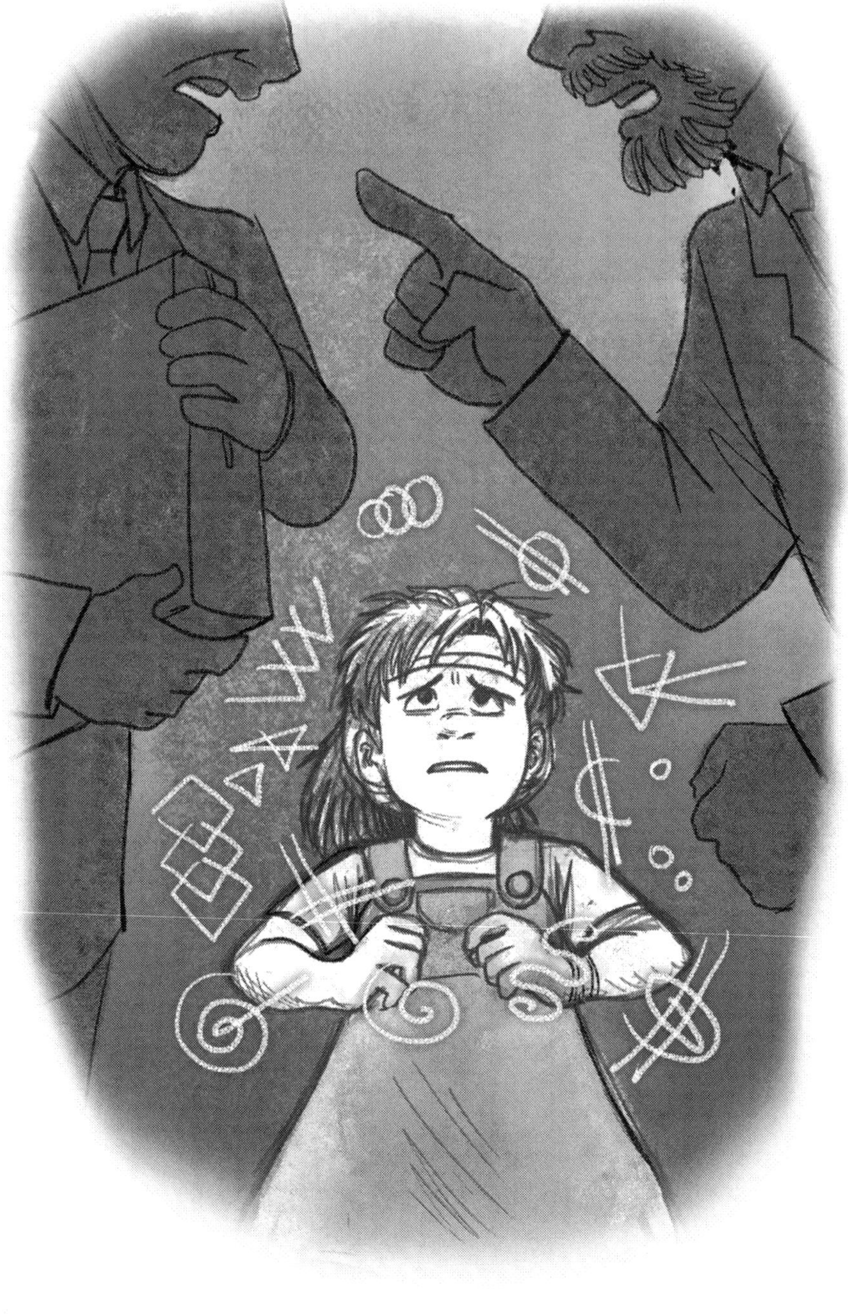

Chapter 8 - A New Plan

compared to what's best for Mason Forge," Dr. Charles said. "Curses cause misfortune, his presence could cause natural disasters or accidents or worse. If you won't let me remove him, I must tell the town he's among them."

"Let me talk to the mayor first," Dad said.

"You can't expect me to keep it quiet."

"Give me one day," Dad said.

Dr. Charles was furious but nodded his head. "One day. That's as long as I'll wait."

"Thank you."

Mom let Dr. Charles out the front door and put her face in her hands. Dad stepped up behind her and whispered something in her ear. Mom looked at him in shock and replied too softly for Cat to hear. Dad nodded and the two hugged tight.

Cat watched Dad's face as he crossed the room. He knelt in front of her chair and took her hands in his. "I know this is all too big for you to understand."

Cat gulped. "Are you going to take Peter to Earth Town like Dr. Charles said?"

"That depends." Dad looked into her eyes. "Do you still want to keep Peter from leaving?"

"Yes! I want that more than anything."

"Then you're going to have to be very

obedient and very brave," Dad said. "You can't draw your shapes, or run away into the woods, or anything to get in trouble. Agreed?"

Cat nodded anxiously.

"And when I ask you to do something, you are going to need to do it just as I say. Is that clear?"

"Yes," Cat said. "Anything for Peter."

"Good. Then, go get some rest," Dad said. "Tomorrow, I'm going to need your help with something very important."

***

Cat had a terrible time sleeping, not because of her floating shapes, but because of nightmares about Peter and running away. In one, the Calligraphers were chasing Cat and Peter with torches. In another, Cat was the Earth Curse and parts of her legs kept crumbling to dust as she tried to run. Cat waited for the the sun to finally rise before getting out of bed. Dad's law books were spread out on the kitchen table.

Mom was wearing the same dress she was wearing the night before. It looked like no one in the family slept well.

Chapter 8 - A New Plan

"Hello, Cat," Mom said.

Mom stacked a couple books to make room for Cat's bowl of breakfast porridge. It was lumpier than usual, but that was okay. Cat didn't feel like eating anyway. "Where's Dad?"

"He had to run an errand."

"To talk to the mayor?"

"I hope so."

One of Cat's phantom shapes settled in her porridge. She traced the lines with her spoon. "Do you think he'll help us?"

Mom took a deep breath and looked like she was going to cry. "Mayor Young is a very nice man, but he also answers to some very important people. It may be out of his control."

"But he's the mayor. He should be in control of everything."

Mom gave an uncomfortable laugh. "This town is a very small part of a much, much, much larger world."

The front door opened and Dad walked in, wearing his best suit and a tie Mom gave him for his birthday. Mom stood up, but Dad spoke to Cat. "Good, you're up."

Hope lit Cat's heart like a lamp. "Will the mayor help?"

"Let's hope so. Get dressed, we need to

75

leave right away."

Cat bit her lip. "And go where?"

"What did I make you promise yesterday?" Dad asked.

Cat jumped from her chair. "Yes, sir!"

Before she knew it, she was wearing her pink "special occasion" dress and walking with Dad up the main street. Cat's heart flit like a caged bird in her chest. Up the hill, the school bell rang. Eric, Jenny, and Brett were waiting on the steps of the school house, but Cat and her father turned left instead of right and headed down a long hill toward City Hall.

Chapter 8 - A New Plan

City Hall was a two-story building made of logs and plaster with a wall-sized carving of the founder of Mason Forge by the front door. The plaque underneath had the date and the man's name: Montgomery.

Cat pointed. "That's Peter's name."

Dad pushed open the door. "Let's hope it does him good."

The front room of City Hall was full of dark wooden furniture and old documents in frames. A patterned rug led to a staircase and up to the second floor where Mayor Young's office waited at the top.

Dad knelt down and pulled Cat close to whisper. "Okay, this is how this is going to go. I need you to be very quiet while I talk, no matter what the mayor says. When I say it's your turn, I want you to tell him about Peter."

Cat was unsure. "What should I say?"

"Whatever your heart feels."

Her chest tightened. The shapes in Cat's eyes quivered.

Dad took her hand. "Let's go."

Chapter 9
The Most Important Meeting

    The staircase felt twice as long and steep as it looked. Cat tightened her grip on Dad's hand as shapes crowded her eyes. They wedged themselves into the rungs of the banister, odd contours in the furniture, and individual letters in the documents framed along the wall. A huge half-circle affixed itself to the wood pattern around the handle of Mayor Young's door. Dad reached through the shape to turn the knob and draw her inside.

Chapter 9 - The Most Important Meeting

The mayor was a farmer before he was a mayor. He was older than Dad with graying sideburns and he wore heavy coveralls over his clean linen shirt. He reached over a pile of papers and books to shake Dad's hand. "You've got ten minutes, Raymond. What was so important that you needed to talk to me?"

"The Montgomery boy is a Curse."

The temperature in the room dropped. Cat's shapes whooshed past her head to the sound of her heartbeat.

Mayor Young stared at Dad, his mouth not quite open. He cleared his throat and tugged the brim of his hat. "Are you sure?"

"Dr. Charles confirmed it," Dad said.

"The baby?"

"No, the older one."

The mayor swore and fell back into his chair. "Poor Sheila, first her husband, now her son in just a couple of years. Rotten luck."

"It doesn't have to be," Dad said.

Mayor Young's eyebrows shot up. "Pardon?"

"I know what the law says about Curses. 'Reject them as you do sin.' It is very clear about that." Dad placed his hands on the mayor's desk. "I'm not here to talk about the law. I want to talk about breaking the law."

Cat's heartbeat doubled. Pride swelled inside her as she watched Mayor Young's eyes widen at the idea, then narrow again with a firm shake of his head.

"Absolutely not. If the Calligraphers catch him here, they'll use their magic against us."

"The Calligraphers haven't been to Mason Forge in ten years," Dad said. "If we don't call them, they'll never come here. We can hide him for the rest of his life."

"What about the misfortune?"

"We'll deal with it," Dad said. "Young, think about what you're asking Sheila to do."

"No less than is asked of the rest of us," the mayor said. "If one of our kids were a Curse, the expectation would be the same."

"He is one of your kids," Dad said. "Maybe in the big city people are okay looking the other way while parents suffer, but this is Mason Forge. The Montgomerys founded this town. We're a family here. We take care of each other."

The mayor's lips pursed, his face reddened. "It's not that simple."

"But it can be." Dad beckoned to Cat.

She took a deep breath, the shapes ran along the pattern of the carpet like ants in an

Chapter 9 - The Most Important Meeting

ant hill. Her feet were heavy as she dragged them to the mayor's massive desk. He rose to look down at her. Cat clawed at the string on her wrist, wishing she could pull it off and fiddle with it to calm down. The shapes snapped to the letters of Mayor Young's name on the front placard.

"I… um…" Cat bit her lip. The shapes vibrated. "Mister Mayor, Peter is my best friend. The Calligraphers say he's a monster but I can tell you he's not. He's smart and funny. He's a good person and he loves me. And I love him, too. I don't want to lose him."

Dad squeezed her shoulder. Mayor Young spoke to her in a kind voice. "Young lady, I know this is hard to cope with, but I have to follow the rules the Calligraphers gave us."

"But sometimes rules aren't fair," Cat said. "Like when Peter fought with Eric on the playground. He didn't sit there and watch me get picked on just because it was against the rules. He always breaks the rules for me."

"There's always an alternative to fighting," Mayor Young said.

"Then what about when we ran away from home last night?" Cat said. Mayor Young looked surprised. She clasped her hands as if

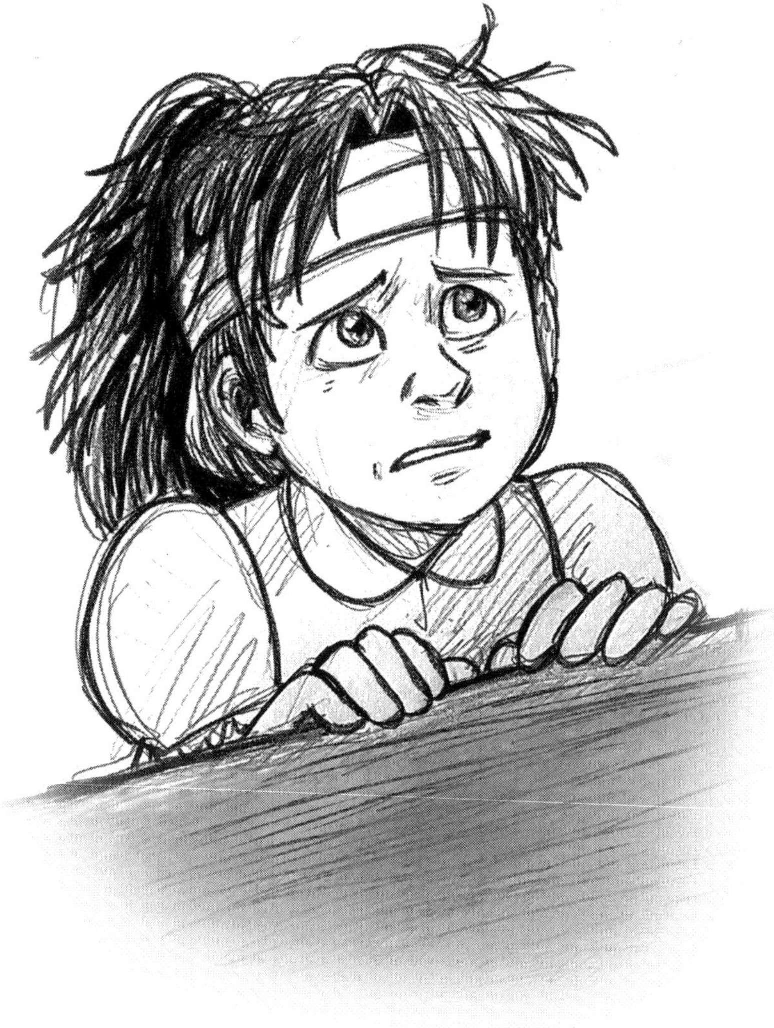

Chapter 9 - The Most Important Meeting

she were praying. "Please. I'm so grounded right now, I probably will never play outside again. But I didn't care how much trouble I got in, if it meant Peter was safe."

Dad petted Cat's hair and spoke. "I know what the law says, but we're talking about a boy's life. Don't cause pain to people who are already hurting."

"He's not a monster," Cat said. "He's a person, all that's changed is that he's sick. If that's enough to throw someone away then get rid of me because I have a bump on my head."

Mayor Young sucked his teeth. He sat back down and folded his hands over the desktop, tapping his thumbs as seconds of silence ticked by. He looked up. "I can't make a choice like this. The town will have to decide."

Dad nodded. "Then give them the opportunity."

The mayor released a long sigh. "I'll call a town meeting."

"Thank you," Dad said. "Let's go, Cat."

She took Dad's hand and left the office. They walked down the stairs and back out to the street. Dad's hand was shaking a little. Cat looked up. "Did it work?"

"I don't know. We'll have to wait and see."

Cat swallowed hard. "Did I help?"

Dad smiled. "Yes, you did great."

They walked up the hill, but instead of turning toward home, Dad dropped Cat off at the schoolhouse door.

"School?" Cat whined. "But I want to stay home with Peter."

"He'll still be there when you get back," Dad promised. "Your mom and I have a lot of work to do today. You're better off here where Mrs. Smith can take care of you."

"I can be home by myself."

"Not right now you can't." He patted her head, making the symbols swirl. "You did a good job at the mayor's office, but that means you need to be extra good in school today. No acting out. You're a character witness for Peter, behave for his sake."

Cat gulped. "If it'll help Peter, I'll work extra hard."

"Good. Don't tell anyone about him. Not until the town meeting." Dad kissed her forehead. "I'm trusting you."

He walked back toward home.

Mrs. Smith was waiting next to Cat's desk when she arrived. "Miss Aston."

"Yes?"

Chapter 9 - The Most Important Meeting

"You ran away from school yesterday."

Cat's stomach turned and her cheeks warmed. "Yes, I did that."

"I cannot even put into words how much trouble you are in."

"It won't happen again," Cat assured. "I promise from the bottom of my heart, no more getting in trouble."

Mrs. Smith looked her up and down skeptically. "I'll give you one more chance. Any more trouble and I'll be talking to your parents about what kind of punishment you'll deserve."

"Yes, ma'am. No more trouble, ma'am."

Mrs. Smith went to the chalk board to begin class. Cat sank into the chair behind her desk, her heart pounding so fast she thought it was going to escape through her ribs. She thought talking to the mayor was scary, but being perfect in class was going to be even harder than that. The shapes flashed in and out of her vision, reminding her how she got in trouble the first time.

She begged them not to do it again.

Chapter 18
Easter

School felt like a prison through the morning classes. Cat did not raise her hand or answer any questions, and didn't have any of her books or homework so she had to borrow paper from Eric who drew a butt on the top. Cat barely noticed it, her thoughts were always on Peter and the meeting the mayor was going to call about his fate.

At recess she was in detention again. She pulled her string off her wrist and started

Chapter 10 - Caster

weaving patterns to get her mind off of worrying.

Cat started with the 'Cup and Saucer' and the 'Calligrapher's Brush,' but the shapes in her eyes kept getting in the way of her patterns. She twisted her fingers new ways and tried to match the patterns she saw with the twists. The challenge of fitting multiple shapes in the web helped settle her stomach, and knowing it wasn't a drawing meant Dad wouldn't get mad.

She managed to get three different shapes locked into the string when Mrs. Smith's shouting caught her attention. All the kids were gathered in a corner of the playground where Mom was standing with Mrs. Montgomery who had Alan on her hip and Peter by her side.

Cat's heart jumped to her throat. She scooted to the end of the bleachers. Peter looked tired with his head hung low and his ankle still wrapped up in bandages. His hand hung limp from his mom's grip, like he had no energy. Cat waved to get his attention, but his eyes were hidden behind his foggy glasses.

"He just has to stay for a short time," Mom said. "The mayor has called a town meeting and Sheila and I need to be there."

Mrs. Smith grimaced. "It's inappropriate. I mean, think of the children…."

"I know you'll keep him safe," Mrs. Montgomery said. "Please. It's very important."

"Alright, he can stay."

Cat scooted back to her spot, her hands bouncing with anticipation. Mrs. Montgomery kissed Peter on both cheeks as she sat him on the bleachers next to Cat. Cat put her hand on Peter's arm. He looked up at her with red, worried eyes.

"Be good, Cat, we'll be right back,"

Chapter 10 - Caster

Mom said. Cat nodded as Mom and Mrs. Montgomery left.

Mrs. Smith cleared her throat and spoke to the whole class. "Everyone needs to come here and pay very close attention."

The few stragglers still playing in the yard came to the bleachers. The air buzzed with a tension that made Cat's chest twinge in anxiety. Shapes quivered before her as she took Peter's arm. He was stiff as a board.

"Everyone listening?" Mrs. Smith said. "I hoped we would be able to address this issue after it was resolved but it appears plans have changed. As a result of yesterday's examination, Mr. Montgomery was revealed to be a Curse."

The kids all gasped. Young Patty's eyes filled with frightened tears. Even Eric looked scared. Peter's cheeks went red as he bowed his head. Cat tightened her grip on his arm.

"The town is currently having a meeting to deal with the problem," Mrs. Smith said. "I know you all know how dangerous being around a Curse is, so for now I want all of you to stay away from it. Don't talk to it or even look at it."

Anger like fire flashed in Cat's chest. She bounded up. "He's not an 'it'!"

Mrs. Smith's nostrils flared. "Catrina, what did we talk about?"

"But he's not an 'it'! He's Peter! Everyone knows Peter."

"Cat," Peter whispered. His voice was trembling. Cat shut her mouth.

Mrs. Smith leveled her finger at Cat. "Move to the other end of the bench."

"But – "

"Do it now, Catrina."

Cat obeyed, her face hot as the sun and her hands in shaking fists. Mrs. Smith turned her back to watch the playground. The kids whispered to each other.

It hurt to see them stare at him with such fear or hatred. The day before, they would have called Peter their friend. They had counted on him to help them with their homework or play with them at recess for as long as they were in school together. Mrs. Smith used to call him her best student, then called him an 'it' in front of everyone.

Cat wanted to scream, but Dad's warning came as clear to her memory as the shapes were in her eyes. She'd been in trouble over and over for Peter's sake. Now for the same reason, she had to be good.

Chapter 10 - Caster

She whispered down the length of the bench as softly as she could, "Pete?"

He didn't answer. A tear dropped from his cheek onto his clasped hands.

Cat's heart pounded. "Pete?"

"Shh!" Mrs. Smith hissed.

Cat looked back at her lap, angrier than ever. She was willing to run away to find him before, but couldn't even talk to him now because of the stupid meeting.

Cat clawed at her string, winding it back onto her hands in attempt to calm herself down. The shapes popped in and out of the web so fast they overlapped. She didn't think about what she was making, just twisted knot after knot. She fit one shape in, then two, then three. Something niggled in the back of her mind, like a memory from long ago, or a song she knew the words to but not the tune. She was too angry to focus on the feeling.

Four shapes fit together in her string when suddenly the white light she'd been seeing in her head was suddenly visible in her hands, and in that same moment all the fire burning in her chest exploded out of the string to coat the ground in front of her in a jet of red flame.

The string fell out of her hands. She

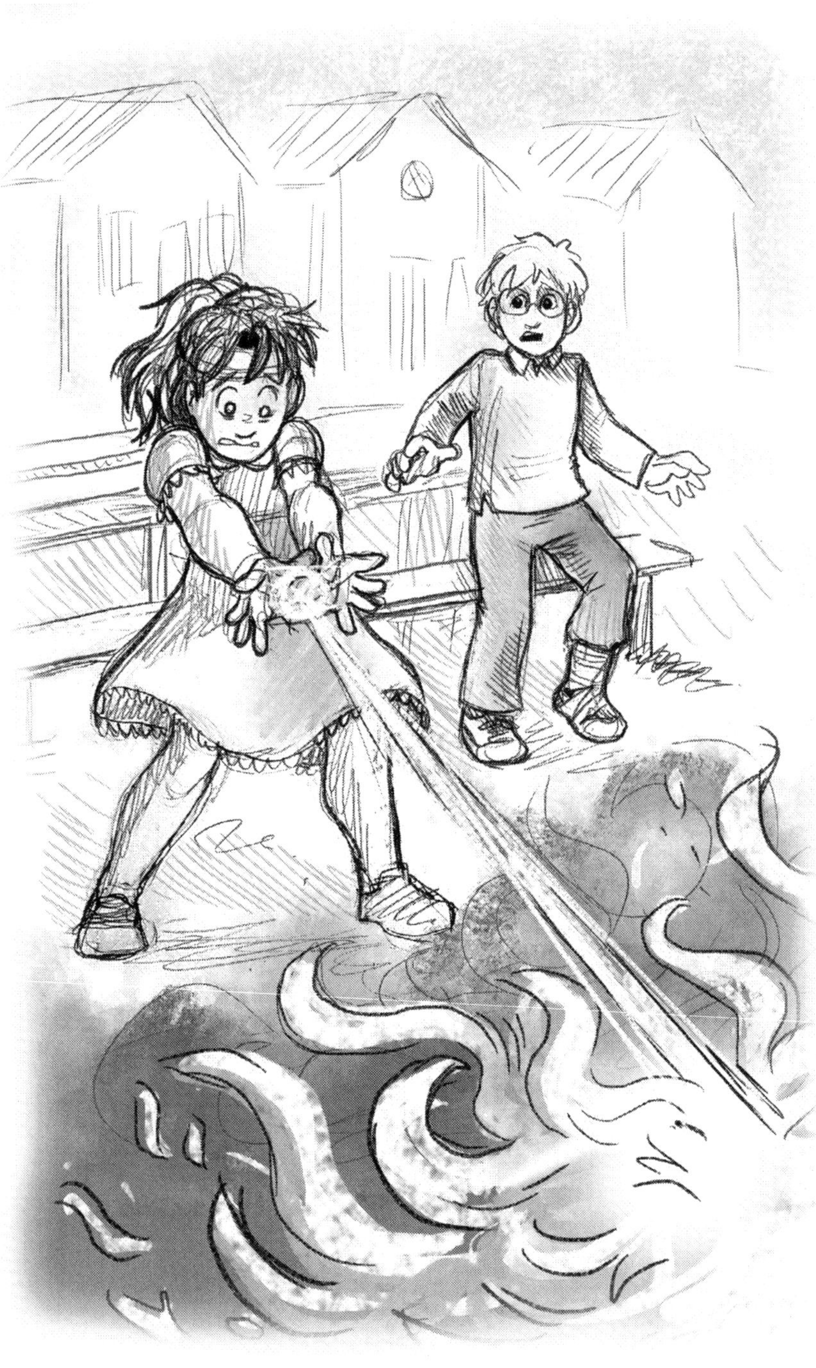

Chapter 10 - Caster

couldn't believe the fire was real, but Peter jumped up and pointed at the flames. "Fire!"

Mrs. Smith turned and stumbled backward in shock. "Eric! Go ring the bell!"

Eric sprinted to the school house as Mrs. Smith hurried the rest of the kids into their fire-drill lines.

Peter stared at Cat. "What happened?"

"I-I don't know!" She gulped. The shapes swarmed in the rising smoke. "Remember when I suggested my shapes were runes like the Calligraphers use to cast spells? I think this proves I was right."

"Hold on," he gaped. "Did you do that?"

She nodded in amazement.

Peter waved his hands in confusion. "You have to put it out!"

"I don't know how to do that!"

"You started it!"

"That doesn't mean I can stop it!" Cat said. "We need water!"

"There's not enough water close by. We need something else." Peter's eyes darted in thought. "Dirt puts out fire!"

"Can you make dirt?" Cat asked. "You know, as an Earth Curse?"

"Only in my bones. We need to use

playground dirt." He pointed across the yard. "The sand box!"

The other students were on their way to the safety of the street. Cat avoided them and grabbed a handful of sand. Peter did the same and limped toward the fire, but it was spreading fast over the dry grass.

"This isn't going to be enough," Cat said. "We need a lot all at once."

The school bell started ringing.

Cat suddenly remembered the trash can she stood on to look in the back window and took off at a run. "I'll be right back!"

The trash can was still where she left it. Cat dragged it back to the playground and turned it on its side. Peter got on his knees and the two started heaping sand in it. When they'd emptied half the sandbox, they dragged the can to the fire and worked together to turn the can of sand over onto the flames.

The sand spilled over the blackened grass and smothered the fire until all that remained was a cloud of white smoke.

Chapter 11
Big Decisions

The school bell had summoned all the townsfolk from the mayor's meeting. Over a hundred people hurried in. Cat didn't know what to do. Peter couldn't run on his ankle and she was too scared to leave him alone, so they stood together in front of the sand pile and waited for them to come.

Mom dashed in first and grabbed Cat in a hug. "Are you okay?"

"I'm fine, Mom."

She was followed by Dad and Mrs. Montgomery who put herself between Peter and the crowd.

"What happened?" Mayor Young asked.

"It just burst into flames!" Mrs. Smith stood in front of the other students like a shield. "Like magic!"

Dad interrupted. "Magic? Nonsense."

"Curses invite misfortune!" Dr. Charles said from within the crowd. "We have to send him away to protect ourselves."

"You're wrong!" Cat yelled. "Peter didn't start the fire!"

Dad turned to her, shocked. "Cat?"

"That's right! Cat did it!" Eric ran out of the school house. He pointed at her. "Mrs. Smith told us to ignore the Curse, but I was watching!"

Dad's brow furrowed. "What did you see?"

"She was playing with matches or something in her hands," Eric said. "She was angry at Mrs. Smith for talking about the Curse, so she tried to set her on fire!"

"I did not!" Cat snapped back, but fear gripped her heart. She was told not to get into trouble, that her behavior protected Peter, but now that Eric had snitched on her, the crowd

Chapter 11 - Big Decisions

was paying attention to her. Cat balled the string in her hand and stood straight and tall. "That's right. The fire was my fault. I didn't mean to do it, but I was angry because of how everyone's been treating Peter."

"Cat, I'm so ashamed of you!" Mom said. "Playing with fire is very dangerous! People could have been hurt."

"I'm sorry, Mom. I didn't want to hurt anyone, but I won't make excuses either," Cat said. "I break rules sometimes, but I own up to my mistakes. You all were ready to blame Peter for the fire because the law said you could, and not because he was guilty. And being sick isn't his fault either. You're trying to punish him for something he didn't do, when he put himself in danger to put the fire out!"

Mrs. Montgomery hugged Peter close. "That was very brave of you, but you should have asked for help instead of trying to handle something like this by yourself."

"Who would help me?" Peter asked, a fresh tear in his eye. "No one even wants to talk to me. But I couldn't let the fire spread to the school or the rest of town. It's too dry out here, everything could burn. I had to do something."

"See? That's bravery," Dad said. "To help

even when no thanks are expected. It's a sign of this boy's true character."

"Peter's not a bad person!" Cat said. "And he's not an 'it' like Mrs. Smith was saying. He's a kid like me, and if you're not going to stand up for him, then I will."

"I will, too," Mom said. "Peter is not a stranger who sneaked into our town overnight. He's a member of our community and we take care of our people here."

The crowd spoke among themselves, but sounded less angry than before. Mayor Young drew their attention. "The question on the table

Chapter 11 - Big Decisions

is do we send Peter to Earth Town like we were told by the Calligraphers, or do we let him stay and take care of him ourselves."

Dr. Charles held his medical bag to his chest as if trying to protect himself. "We've never dealt with something like this before. What if it does lead to misfortune?"

"Then we will deal with it the way we've dealt with the drought, or the dying trees, or the dry river," Dad said. "Misfortune happened long before Peter was born and we survived just fine because the people of Mason Forge stick together."

"I don't want to betray one of our own," Dr. Charles said. "But the Calligraphers were clear about what we should do."

"Who cares what outsiders think!" A man called from the back. The other townsfolk laughed and the tension in the air eased.

Dad grinned. "We in Mason Forge have always supported each other. If we stop now, we'll sacrifice a big part of who we are."

The rest of the crowd murmured, their voices less afraid and more curious. Mayor Young raised his hand. "Okay, everyone in favor of keeping Peter say 'aye'!"

The "aye"s were few at first, but gained

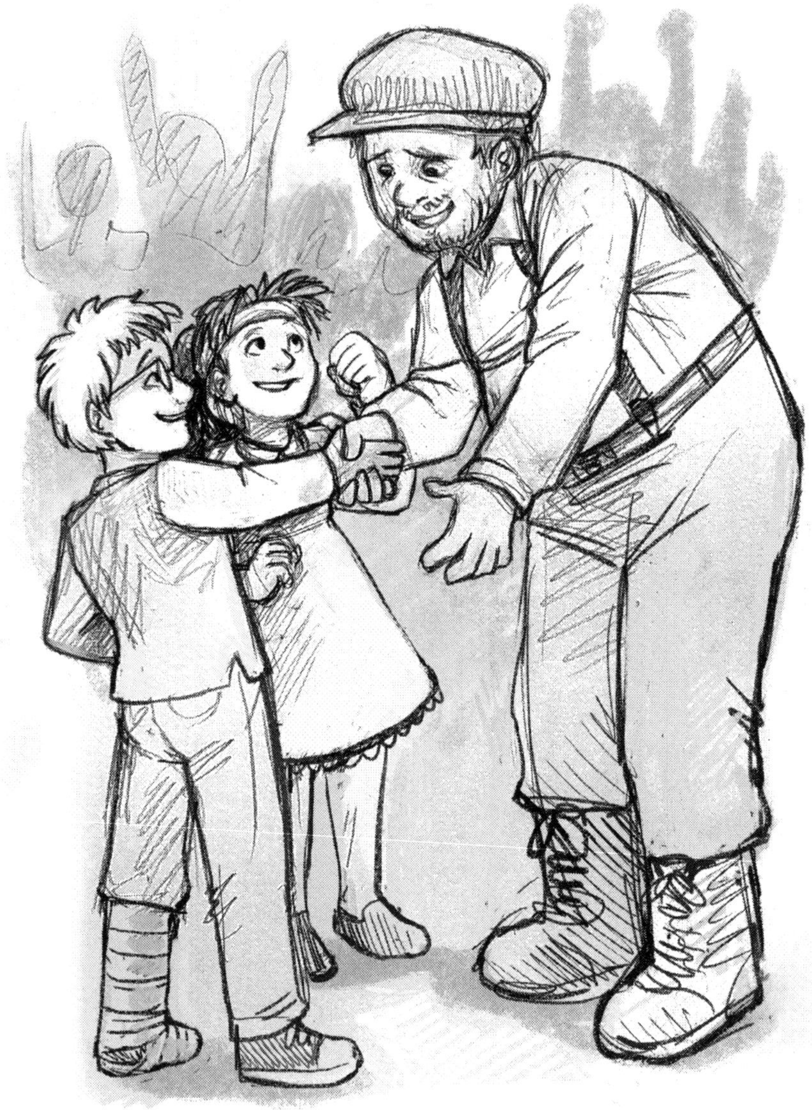

Chapter 11 - Big Decisions

strength as the townsfolk heard their neighbors agree. Mom, Dad, and Sheila added their "aye"s, as did Mrs. Smith and Dr. Charles. Soon a hundred voices called out in approval.

Mayor Young nodded. "All right. Everyone who is against it say 'nay'!"

"Nay!" One voice said.

Cat turned to see Eric pouting with his arms crossed. She snapped at him. "Eric! How can you say 'no'?"

"Because you guys set the yard on fire and got away with it!" Eric replied. "If I did that I'd be in detention forever!"

"I'm sure she'll get detention enough," Mayor Young chuckled. He stepped forward and patted Peter on the back. "If there are no further objections, I declare this meeting adjourned. Congratulations, young man, it looks like you can stay."

Peter smiled a broad, toothy grin. "Thank you, Mister Mayor!"

Mrs. Montgomery swept her son up in a hug, kissing and cuddling him in pure joy. Mom and Dad embraced.

"And congratulations to you, too, Miss Aston," Mayor Young said.

Cat gasped. "Me?"

"Yes." The mayor knelt down and took her shoulders. "Your loyalty and dedication to your friend changed my mind, and now it's changed the minds of everyone else. It's important to obey the rules, but it's even more important to do the right thing. I'm sorry you felt you had to act out to get attention."

"I'm sorry for setting the playground on fire," Cat said. "It was wrong of me to do."

"I think Mrs. Smith will forgive you." Mayor Young looked back at the teacher.

Mrs. Smith's face reddened. "I…. I suppose the last couple of days have been a bit of an extraordinary circumstance. Perhaps tomorrow we can start fresh, but she still has detention for misbehaving."

Cat shrugged. "That's fair. I mean, I did start a fire."

"You did, yes," Dad said. He gave Cat a severe and disapproving look.

A knot tightened in her throat. She had a feeling she was going to be grounded for a very, very long time.

Chapter 12: The Secret of the Shapes

That night, Mrs. Montgomery threw a party for Peter. Cat and her parents brought the leftover roast from Cat's "get well" dinner over to the Montgomery's house and Mrs. Montgomery baked a huge cake like it was Peter's birthday.

"Because I feel like I got you back today," she said and lit a candle on top of the cake.

Peter grinned and blew the candle out and

everyone cheered. Cat ate a huge slice of cake and played board games with Peter and their parents until it was time for Alan to go to bed. It was so much fun that Cat forgot about setting the fire at school until they got home.

"Cat," Dad said.

He was using his disciplinary voice. Cat bit her lip and held her arms tight to her sides. "Yes, sir."

"The fire," he lowered his voice to a whisper. "The teacher said it was like magic."

Cat grimaced. "Something like that."

Dad took her arms and steered her to the couch where they sat down. He leaned even closer to whisper. "Tell me what happened."

"I… um," Cat stammered. "It's the shapes."

"Yes?"

"You told me not to draw them on paper anymore," Cat said. "So I twisted them in my string. I didn't mean to start a fire. It just kind of happened."

"Do you remember the shape you used?"

"No, it was a bunch of shapes all at once," Cat said. "Do you know what they are?"

"I do. Those shapes are the runes the Calligraphers use to do magic."

"I knew it!" Cat couldn't help smiling.

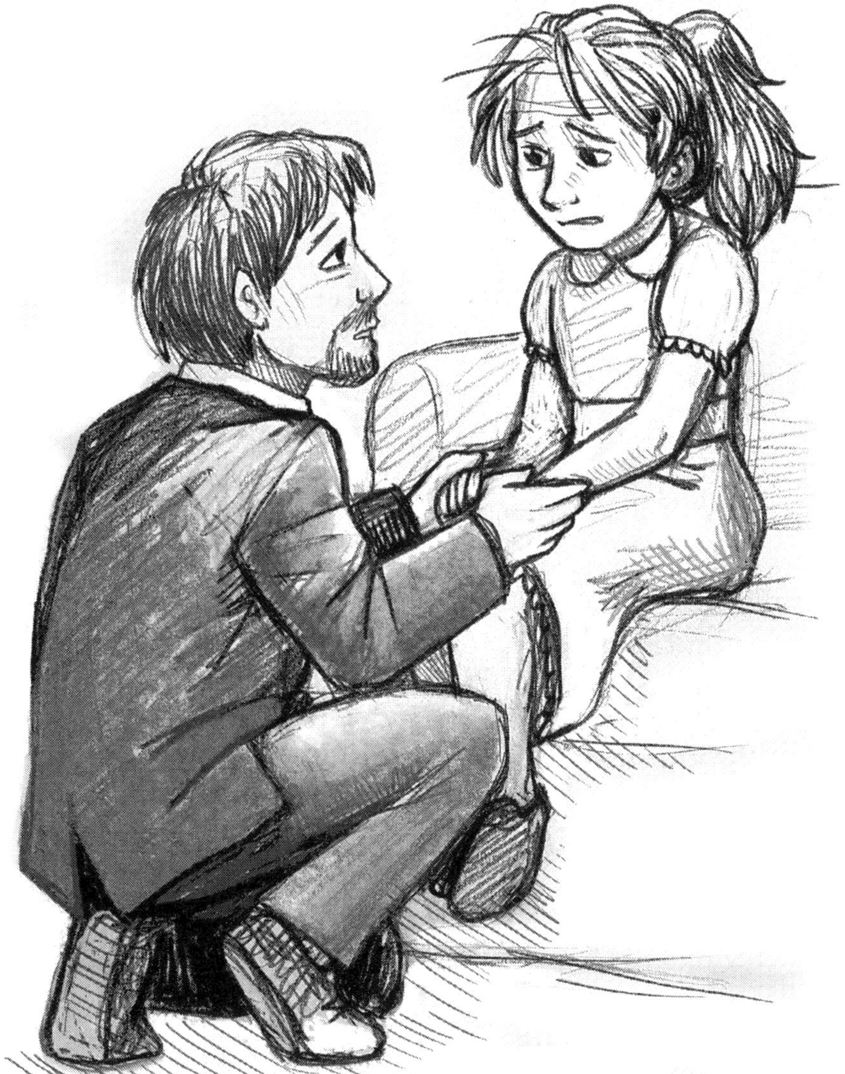

"But what are they doing in my head?"

"I can't say," Dad said. "All I can tell you is that the shapes are special, and should not be shared. That's why I tore your drawing up. If other people saw them, there would be a lot of trouble for both of us. Especially you. You could go to jail for it."

"I don't want that."

"Neither do I. I've learned a lot about you this week, Cat. I've learned you're very smart, but also very stubborn and very headstrong. You protected Peter with everything you had, and didn't hesitate to do what was right even when you were told not to." Dad took her hand. "I'm not punishing you for using the shapes, but I'm trusting you to do the right thing about this. Don't show anyone else the shapes you've seen, not even your mom, and don't use them like you did today. They're our secret, okay?"

Cat thought a moment. When Dad sent her to her room for drawing the shapes, she didn't think it was fair, but now that he was trusting her with a secret it felt different.

She'd learned a lot about him in the last couple of days, too. He kept his promise to help, and she was proud of him for standing up for Peter in front of the whole town. He wanted

Chapter 12 - The Secret of the Shapes

what was best for her, and wouldn't ask her to keep a secret if it wasn't important.

Cat nodded. "I promise."

"Thank you," Dad said. "Now go to bed. We won a victory today, but the challenges are just starting for both you and Peter. You'll need a good night's rest."

"Okay. Goodnight, Dad." Cat hopped from the couch and trotted to the kitchen. "Goodnight, Mom."

"Goodnight, dear!" She kissed Cat's head and removed the white bandage. "It looks like your bump has finally gone away."

Cat pressed a hand to her forehead, but the shapes didn't appear. Her heart swelled. After a week seeing the shapes, following their direction, and using them to cast magic she almost missed not seeing them, but she knew they were still a part of her. Cat brushed her teeth and closed her bedroom door before opening her window and dropping out into the yard.

A lot had changed for Cat and Peter, but their adventures together had just begun.

THE END

Thank you for reading Shapecaster!
This is part of a wide universe of books!
check www.threadcaster.com
for news on more books for all ages
by Jennifer Stolzer!

About the Author:

Jennifer Stolzer is an author/illustrator living and working in St. Louis Missouri. Trained as an animator, she does her best to put life and color into all her characters. When she's not working on her own books, she illustrates books for others and serves as secretary in the St. Louis Writer's Guild.

Made in the USA
Columbia, SC
26 February 2022